"I'm the boss.
I can't take advantage of you."

Rafe threw back his head and laughed. "So what does that mean?" he asked as they got into the elevator car. "I have to wait until Monday before I can attempt any sort of intimacy with you, no matter how innocent?"

"Hmm." Shelley pretended to think about it. They reached their floor and got off, and she started toward her hotel room. "No. Sorry. That won't work, either."

Reaching into her pocket, she produced her plastic room card and pushed it into the slot. "On Monday, the inappropriateness turns in the other direction, and it would be *you* taking advantage of me."

Her door opened and she turned to smile impishly at him.

His answering grin was endearingly lopsided as he leaned with one arm against her doorway....

Dear Reader,

Saying goodbye is never easy, and when "goodbye" means leaving a line I've come to love, farewell is even harder. I hope you have enjoyed Silhouette Romance under my leadership and continue to cherish this terrific line under the direction of Ann Leslie Tuttle, Silhouette Romance's new associate senior editor.

And if you're looking for a handsome hero, look no further than Silhouette Romance! From bosses to princes to cowboys to oilmen, you'll find a man for every woman's taste this month.

He's a prince disguised as a sexy American executive; she's a princess disguised as his hotel manager. Don't miss Princess Meredith's last matchmaking attempt—for herself!— in *Twice a Princess* (SR #1758) by Susan Meier, the conclusion to the miniseries IN A FAIRY TALE WORLD....

Trading Places with the Boss (SR #1759) was supposed to be a learning experience. But what this secretary finds is an alarming attraction to her employer—and he seems to feel it, too! Raye Morgan brings us an office romance to remember in the latest book in her BOARDROOM BRIDES miniseries.

When this city girl escaped to the country to mend her broken heart, she finds herself face-to-face with temptation: an ex-rodeo rider working on the neighboring ranch. Will she give in? Find out in Madeline Baker's *Every Inch a Cowboy* (SR #1760).

Two star-crossed soul mates get some heavenly help with their love lives in Debrah Morris's *A Little Night Matchmaking* (SR #1761). This West Texas oilman is always all-business, until he meets his match in a feisty single mom.

May this month's heroes lead you into a world of true love and happily-ever-after.

Sincerely,

Mavis C. Allen
Associate Senior Editor

Please address questions and book requests to:
Silhouette Reader Service
U.S.: 3010 Walden Ave., P.O. Box 1325, Buffalo, NY 14269
Canadian: P.O. Box 609, Fort Erie, Ont. L2A 5X3

Trading Places with the Boss

RAYE
MORGAN

SILHOUETTE *Romance*®

Published by Silhouette Books

America's Publisher of Contemporary Romance

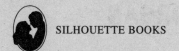 SILHOUETTE BOOKS

ISBN 0-373-19759-4

TRADING PLACES WITH THE BOSS

Copyright © 2005 by Helen Conrad

This edition published by arrangement with Harlequin Books S.A.

® and TM are trademarks of Harlequin Books S.A., used under license. Trademarks indicated with ® are registered in the United States Patent and Trademark Office, the Canadian Trade Marks Office and in other countries.

Visit Silhouette Books at www.eHarlequin.com

Printed in U.S.A.

RAYE MORGAN

has spent almost two decades, while writing over fifty novels, searching for the answer to that elusive question: Just what is that special magic that happens when a man and a woman fall in love? Every time she thinks she has the answer, a new wrinkle pops up, necessitating another book! Meanwhile, after living in Holland, Guam, Japan and Washington, D.C., she currently makes her home in Southern California with her husband and two of her four boys.

Chapter One

"Here we go," Shelley Sinclair whispered to the co-worker sitting next to her in the plush seats of the auditorium.

Jaye Martinez nodded and gave her a quick grin.

Shelley took a deep breath, closed her eyes for luck, and opened the folded paper she'd been handed.

Allman Industries, Team A
Role exchangers: Rafe Allman and Shelley Sinclair

She stared at the notation in dismay. *No! Not Rafe Allman!*

Jaye glanced at her own paper, then leaned close to see Shelley's. Her eyes widened and she whispered teasingly, "Whatever you do, don't show fear. Men like that can sense it, like dogs, and they'll rip you apart."

Still reeling from the horrifying partner she'd been given in the conference competition, Shelley didn't get it right away.

"What?" she said.

Laughing, Jaye patted her arm. "I'm only kidding. Rafe Allman isn't really that bad. In fact, he's about the hunkiest boss in this part of Texas, so you ought to be able to put up with a little arrogance if that comes with the deal."

"Speak for yourself," Shelley muttered, looking over to see who Jaye had drawn. Then she sighed, completely jealous and careless about showing it. "You got Mr. Tanner. He's such a sweetie—you'll have a great time with him."

Jaye nodded happily. "I'm already planning ways to wrap him around my little finger. I've got four whole days to convince him I'm the only woman in the world made just for him. What kind of odds will you give me?"

Shelley managed a wistful smile, looking at her beautiful friend whose raven tresses were a direct contrast to her own long blond hair.

"He's a goner. No doubt about it."

Jaye put on an innocent look, making Shelley grin. Then she rose, joining the throngs of others leaving the auditorium. Shelley gathered her conference bag and the stack of handouts and followed her. As their crowd emptied into the foyer of the luxury hotel where the conference was being held, she caught sight of Rafe Allman and Jim Tanner waiting for them at the bottom of the ramp.

She groaned—partly because she dreaded meeting up with her assigned partner, and partly because she hated the way her heart began to pound out a nervous rhythm at the prospect. Even so, the crush of people was slowing progress long enough for her to make a studied comparison of the two men.

Jim Tanner was tall and blond with a twinkle in his eye and a face that looked ready to smile. Rafe Allman was a different sort entirely. Just as tall, his shoulders were square and broad giving him a look of strength Jim Tanner just didn't have. His dark eyes had a searching look and his face seemed more ready to twist with cynicism than to smile.

And still, he was devastatingly, head-turningly handsome. Countless women would have jumped at the chance to spend four days in close contact with the man.

Unfortunately she wasn't one of them. Maybe she'd known him too long—and knew enough to stay away. She'd always thought there was something wild in Rafe, like an animal that had been gentled, but never tamed.

His head went back as he spotted the two women. He gave Jaye a welcoming smile, but that smile dimmed a bit as he made eye contact with Shelley. She lifted her chin. That was fine with her. They were going to have to work together, but that didn't mean she was ready to let down any safeguards.

Rafe was the de facto head of Allman Industries, a

distribution center for local Texas wineries, even though his father was still the actual president of the company. And Rafe fulfilled the role of the man in charge with cool assurance.

"Like lambs to the slaughter," Jaye said under her breath just before they met the men.

"Who? Us or them?" Shelley was afraid that she and Jaye had a slightly different perspective on the matter.

"You missed the introductory address," Jaye told the men as they met them, her tone accusing but also just this side of flirtatious. "You missed all the information about what we're supposed to do."

"That's what we have you lovely ladies here for," Rafe said with a humorous gleam in his eye. "We're counting on your legendary attention to detail."

"We'll share the burden," Shelley said lightly. "Next meeting, you two can attend, and Jaye and I will play hooky."

Rafe raised one silky dark eyebrow, looking surprised. Did he think she was being a bit presumptuous, considering he was the highest-ranking Allman Industries executive here and she was a lowly administrative assistant? Little did he know that situation was about to make a radical change. Her pulse was racing at the thought.

Her gaze met his and caught for just a beat or two, and suddenly she knew it was more than her attitude he was aware of. He was thinking back to last New Year's Eve when, for just a moment, the possibility of something romantic had sparked between them. It hadn't lasted long, and they had both spent the rest of the year avoiding each other like the plague, despite the fact that they worked for the same company. But it was always there between them, every time they met.

"We've got a table in the bar," Jim Tanner was saying. "Come on and fill us in over drinks."

Jaye very happily took his arm and began teasing him about how surprised he was going to be when he found out what the theme of the contest was this year. That left Shelley and Rafe to walk stiffly side by side, each trying to ignore the other.

The bar was noisy and crowded but the table was being saved by a couple of other employees from Allman Industries and soon they were all six jammed around it. Shelley talked and laughed with the others as they ordered drinks, but she noted that Rafe had very carefully taken a seat as far away from her as he could get.

"Well, I really wish someone would explain to me exactly what we're doing here," Dorie Berger, a pert young office worker, said plaintively. "Everyone keeps telling me this is such a privilege to get to attend, but no one ever bothered to fill me in on what goes on at these things."

"This is the way it works," Rafe said, giving her a smile that seemed to Shelley to be mostly about showing his admiration for Dorie's tight-fitting sweater. "The competition is in a different city each year. Each company is allowed to submit up to three teams made up of seven of their employees each. They all spend the four days of the conference getting their presentation honed and ready. On the last day, each team does its thing in front of the judges and the winner gets a nice big trophy for the trophy case at work—and the prestige that goes with it in the industry."

"But what's the point?" Dorie asked, still looking bewildered.

"It's supposed to make us think outside of the box and come up with new ideas," Jim Tanner offered. "The point is to encourage us all to strive for excellence in our business dealings."

"Not quite," Rafe said deliberately, and suddenly everyone was quiet, listening to him.

That very fact alone drove Shelley wild. Why did they all act like he was the most marvelous thing since the invention of the wheel? He was just a very handsome, very dynamic, very charismatic—regular guy. That was all.

"The point," he was saying dramatically, "is to give the best damn presentation in the competition. The point is to grind your competitors in the dust. The point…" He raised his glass and looked around the table, his own dark eyes hinting at a steely determination. "The point is to win."

"Hear, hear," said Jaye, and they clinked glasses all around.

Shelley joined them, but her heart wasn't in it. Taking on the leadership role here was going to thrust her into a position she might not like very much. She was going to have to fight Rafe all the way. Was she really ready for this?

Quickly she shoved that thought aside. She would have to think about that later, when she was alone. Right now dealing with being at a table under the direct observation of Rafe's too-knowing gaze was about as much as she could handle.

"Well, what are the competitions like?" Dorie was asking.

"It's different every year," Jim said. "One year you had to pretend your product was a politician and develop an election campaign around it. Campaign signs and speeches."

Shelley smiled, then offered up, "Last year we had to develop a ten-minute musical for our product, with each person on the team singing something for at least one minute."

"Oh, no!"

"Did we win?" Rafe asked, gazing at her levelly.

Shelley hesitated. "I think the A team came in fifth." She saw his look of disapproval and she bristled. "That's not so bad. There were ninety-two teams competing."

His gaze sharpened. "So you came last year? I thought this gig was on a three-year rotation."

Attendance was considered a perk and company policy was that each employee could only do it once every three years so that the spots were shared more equally around the workforce.

"Yes, I came last year," she admitted. "Actually, Harvey Yorgan was supposed to come with you all today, but his wife went into premature labor, so I got volunteered at the last minute."

Actually, she'd volunteered herself, and with an ulterior motive that she couldn't reveal to anyone. But that was something she hoped no one would figure out, most of all, Rafe Allman.

"Well, we're down to the wire," he said, looking at her expectantly. "Let's have it. What is it this year?"

She licked her dry lips. "This year one member of the squad has to change places with the boss."

He stared at her as though he didn't understand what she was saying, so she amplified.

"The highest ranking person on each team has to become just one of the employees," she explained. "And one of the employees becomes the new boss."

The air seemed still between them as he digested this setup. Then he shrugged.

"Great." Rafe gave her a comical grin. "So I don't have to do any work."

Everybody laughed. Everybody but Shelley. He was still staring into her eyes, and she was staring right back. She was not going to let him intimidate her. But her heart was still pounding.

"So who is it?" he asked at last, but surely he already guessed.

"Jaye will be trading with Jim." She smiled at her friend, then glanced at Rafe. "And you and I will be switching," she added, trying not to sound as breathless as she felt.

He cocked an eyebrow. "Interesting."

Something in his voice—and his eyes—sent a shiver slithering down her spine.

"*Don't show fear,*" Jaye had said. She'd been joking, but she'd been closer to the mark than she knew. Shelley had to admit it, if only to herself. The man scared her.

Not in a physical way. She didn't suspect he had an abusive side. But there was a streak of animal magnetism to him that sent her over the moon. Maybe it was just a quirk in her own character. Maybe she had a natural weakness for men with midnight eyes and chiseled chins, like some women had a weakness for wine or chocolate. Whatever—she knew she was drawn to him, and she also knew giving in to that pull would be very bad for her.

"Then what do we do?" he asked at last. "Learn to tap dance to our company theme song?"

Her smile was tight. "We develop a business plan that will enhance the operations of our company in some way."

His gaze became speculative. "You mean besides providing a product along with jobs and benefits for our employees and making a little profit off the top."

"Yes."

"Right." He grinned and leaned back in his chair, taking a sip of his drink. Then he looked at them all with a reassuring smile. "Don't worry. I'll handle this."

That did it! How could she be so attracted to a man

who made her so angry at the same time? The conde-
scending tone did it for her. It conjured up too many
memories of times in the past when he'd tormented her
in one way or another. Reaching into one of her Quality in Performance and Leadership Conference folders,
she pulled out the information sheet and put it in front
of him so that he could see the setup for himself.

"Actually, *I'll* be handling it," she told him as calmly
as she could manage. "And the first decision I'm making is to have a strategy meeting."

He looked surprised. "What for?"

Oh, he was going to be tough. She could see it right
now. He wasn't going to give up the reins of power
without a fight. There was no way he was going to submit peacefully. But he was going to have to.

"We need to get going on a project right away," she
said quickly. "Five o'clock. My room. Please let the others know, Rafe. The list of our group members is attached." She smiled at him, trying to maintain a
professional air despite the fact that she was furious
with him. "Your first assignment."

His eyes narrowed. Shelley had a sense of everyone
else at the table holding their breath, waiting to see what
was going to happen next. She had to make a move before he did.

Grabbing her purse, conference bag and papers, she
rose from her chair.

"Oh, and Rafe?" she said, turning back, her heart
beating hard in her chest. "For the next four days, why

don't you call me Miss Sinclair? That might help you keep our new positions straight."

She smiled sweetly at everyone, noting the stunned faces all around, and then her gaze came back to meet Rafe's. Was that anger she saw? Laughter? Mockery?

She couldn't tell. But there was no time for analysis. If she delayed this dramatic leave-taking any longer, she would spoil the whole thing.

"See you at five," she said, turning to go.

She didn't hear what he said, but she recognized his low voice saying something, and the table erupted with laughter just as she reached the doorway. Had he been making fun of her? No doubt. Her face was suddenly very hot and she knew she must be glowing like a neon sign.

"Darn you, Rafe Allman," she muttered to herself as she went quickly toward the elevator. "Darn you and the horse you rode in on!"

Five o'clock came and Shelley waited nervously, adjusting chairs, turning down the music. What if Rafe defied her and didn't show up? What if he didn't tell the others? What if he did show up and made fun of her all through the meeting?

Think it couldn't happen? Hah!

The thing was, she and Rafe had a track record that went back over twenty years. There were times when her close friendship with his sister Jodie meant that she had practically lived at the Allman house. Growing up, her mother had been busy all the time with the coffee shop she ran, Millie's Café. On hot summer days, Shelley usually found her way to Jodie's and the two of them did all the things young girls frolicked in together.

Even back then she and Rafe had been adversaries. He was always finding some way to embarrass her or make her feel inadequate. He was, after all, the one who pointed out to everyone at the Allman dinner table when she was eleven and wore her first training bra to dinner at their house. Her face still burned when she thought of the looks on all their faces as they stared in surprise and amusement at her youthfully modest chest.

Too bad she didn't find a way to murder him then.

Never mind. She was stuck with him for the weekend so she would just have to make the best of it. She knew he must hate her in the position of being his boss, even if temporarily. And she knew she was going to have to fight him all the way just to keep him from taking over.

If only Rafe's older brother Matt had come instead of Rafe. Matt was older, wiser…nicer. She considered him the ideal big brother she never really had. She would do just about anything for him.

A knock sounded and she jumped. Taking a deep breath, she walked quickly to the door and opened it.

"Good evening, *Miss Sinclair.*" Rafe stood looking down at her, the mockery in his eyes echoing the mockery in his voice.

Behind him was the rest of the group. She did a quick inventory. Candy Yang, a paralegal, would make a great assistant. She'd dealt with her before. Jerry was head of finance, but she also knew he was a home carpenter who loved woodworking and could easily supervise building sets. Pretty little Dorie Berger was an entry-level office worker, a sweet young thing who would do pretty much as she was told. And the two others were people she didn't really know very well, but they seemed agreeable.

"Here we are," Rafe was saying, draping himself across her doorway. "Your loyal minions, awaiting your command."

"Good," she said, standing back. "Come on in. We need to get started right away."

Her gaze met his as he sauntered into the room. Something hard and challenging lurked deep in his eyes, and her mouth went dry as she noted it. The weekend was going to be a rough one. Her challenge had only begun.

Chapter Two

Sometimes that whole damn sex thing just got in the way.

Rafe sat toying with the remains of a sumptuous dessert, moving curled pieces of bitter chocolate from one side of the plate to the other with his silver fork. But his mind was on the woman at the other end of the long table.

Shelley Sinclair. He'd known her just about all his life. And here she was, complicating things for him once again. It would certainly be easier if she didn't have that long, silky hair that fell down into a sensual curl just over the swell of her left breast. If she didn't have those doe-shaped eyes that seemed to hide a secret sorrow. If she didn't have that soft, lush mouth that always made him think of long, hot kisses and the scent of gardenias.

Why gardenias? He had no idea.

And the entire thing disgusted him anyway. Just looking at her now, as she slowly put another forkful of whipped cream in that beautiful mouth, he felt a surge of desire that almost made him groan aloud. He was too old for this sort of thing, dammit! Lusting after anyone would have been a problem, but lusting after Shelley Sinclair was nuts.

It hadn't always been like this. Years ago, when Shelley had hung around the Allman house with his little sister Jodie, and the two of them had spied on him and teased him and made his life miserable, he certainly hadn't thought of her as sexy. In fact, if he thought of her at all, it had been with extreme annoyance—as in, "What a brat!"

But that was then.

Now she was another sort of irritant. And he couldn't let that get in the way of what had to be accomplished here. He hadn't asked for this assignment, but now that it had been thrust on him, he was damn well going to come out of it with a trophy in his hand. Allman Industries had to win this competition and it was up to him to make sure that happened. This whole setup, where he was supposed to switch places with Shelley, was going to work against him having the control he needed. And he was going to have to do something about that.

The strategy meeting had been frustrating. He'd assumed that after a little bit of moderating for window-dressing, she would gracefully sit back and let him take over. After all, that was where he belonged, where he usually was—in charge. It was the natural order of things and everyone knew it.

Everyone but Shelley, who seemed to be on another trajectory entirely. She'd held onto the floor, stubborn as a squirrel with the last fall acorn. She had plans and she laid them out, talking fast, assigning workshops for the next morning, giving out instruction sheets. He'd hardly gotten a word in edgewise.

And just when he'd had enough and he'd stood up to take over the reins by force if he had to, she'd given him a triumphant look and adjourned for dinner. Then they had all trooped down to the restaurant to meet the other Allman Industries employees for a totally choice meal. All twenty-one of them. Made you wonder who was home minding the store.

But that was okay. This competition was important, more important than the others here knew. It wasn't just his competitive nature that was at stake here. A major supply contract hinged on the outcome. That was the way they had built the business, scraping and fighting for every advantage. He'd promised his father he would deliver a win and that was what he was going to do. After all, if he was going to prove to them all that he was the natural pick to take over the company, he had to show that he could be just as ruthless as his father ever was.

The others were rising from the table, preparing to go back to their rooms and get some sleep before attending the workshops in the morning. Rafe rose, too, nodding to Jim but brushing aside a melting look from Tina, the raven-haired, statuesque director of personnel who had been giving him the come-on for weeks now, and he headed straight for Shelley.

She looked up, surprised, when he took her arm and leaned close.

"We need to talk," he said softly near her ear.

Her lovely mouth tilted at the corners. "Talk is cheap," she quipped, gathering her things and looking toward the exit. "Send me an e-mail."

His fingers ringed her upper arm. He wasn't about to let her bolt, despite the way her flesh felt under his hand.

"You want all communications in writing, so you can hold my words as evidence against me?" he responded in kind. "Just a bit too transparent, Shelley. I'm not going to fall for that one."

"Too smart for me, huh?" She gave a significant glance at his hand on her arm. "Or, if brains don't work for you, you're ready to move on to manhandling. Is that it?"

He didn't let go. "Intimidation can come in many forms," he noted dryly. "Some of them just your size."

"Are you accusing me of using my feminine wiles to intimidate you?" she said, looking more amused than anything else.

He opened his mouth to say something that would get him into a lot of trouble, but luckily, he thought better of it in time.

"Shelley, I just want to talk to you. Don't make a federal case out of it."

"Okay." She made a face that made it obvious she was surrendering to the inevitable. "Come on up to my room. I'll give you fifteen minutes."

Rafe drew in a deep breath, looking down at her. Okay, here was the crux of his dilemma. Every part of him yearned toward an evening alone in her room. He could already see the soft light, feel the romantic music coming in over the sound system, taste the way her mouth would yield under his….

No way. Couldn't be done. How about the bar?

The music there would be throbbing with sensual urgency, the atmosphere provocative, the sense of impending possibilities tantalizing, her mouth would be just as tempting—and alcohol would be involved.

No. Too dangerous.

"Let's walk down to the canal," he said quickly, deciding a public walkway filled with tourists would pose the least risk. "Soak up some of the ambience."

A slight frown appeared, but she nodded. "Fine. Let's go."

The evening air was unusually warm. The crowd was thick and in a rollicking mood. Lights from the boutiques and clubs bounced off the water and laughter formed a foundation for the music that filled the night. The scene was celebration.

But Rafe felt edgy. He shoved his hands into the pockets of his jacket to keep from reaching out to help guide Shelley as she walked along beside him. Glancing sideways he saw that she came up above his shoulder. The perfect fit for him. He could already feel how it would be to put an arm around her slender form and curl her up against him.

He swore softly, fed up with the way his mind kept trending.

"You rang?" she said quizzically, glancing upwards in a way that emphasized the almond shape of her big brown eyes, her dark lashes leaving long shadows on her cheeks.

He swallowed hard and looked to the heavens for help. "Sorry," he said shortly. "I just had a thought."

"Quite an unusual experience for you I guess," she said archly. "Do you swear every time you get one of those?"

He stared at her, fighting off the impulse to grab her and either shake her or kiss her. "You know what?" he said instead. "You're as big a brat now as you were when we were kids."

She glared at him. "Why not? You're as big a bully."

The crowd surged around them and someone bumped against Shelley, sending her reeling into his arms.

"Sorry," said a disembodied voice but Rafe's first instinct to go after the perpetrator evaporated as he looked down into her face and felt the fragility of her body against the strength of his.

Time stood still. He couldn't breathe. The background faded into a swirling mist and all he could see were her huge eyes.

Then things went back to normal and they pulled

apart, avoiding each other sternly, walking quickly toward the river. Rafe turned into a viewing bump-out and she settled alongside him as he leaned his elbows on the railing and stared into the inky waters below.

It was too late to pretend he didn't react to her like a bug on a hot skillet. Everything she did, every time she moved, everything she said, triggered a response in him of one kind or another. If he couldn't conquer it, at least he had to learn to hide it. He stood very still, steeling himself. Time to take back the controls, all the way around. Otherwise he was going to turn into a mushy mess. And that couldn't happen.

Shelley was floundering. She had no idea what was going on with Rafe. He was acting so weird. He probably hated her.

And why not? She'd never liked him much.

Of course, there had been that New Year's Eve party when they had both had a little too much to drink. He'd hung around making caustic comments and she'd given as good as she got—but when midnight came, he'd kissed her. The surprise of that kiss had shocked them both and they'd drawn apart unable to look each other in the eye. If it had been anyone else, that kiss might have launched a torrid affair. But since it was the two of them, they hadn't spoken to each other since—until this weekend. The fact was, any sort of civil relationship between them just wasn't meant to be.

Sighing, she looked out at the water, enjoying the bobbing lights reflected there. A slight breeze pressed the lacy fabric of her skirt against her legs.

"I love San Antonio," she murmured, mostly to herself as she drew her shawl closer around her shoulders.

He turned to look at her, then looked away again.

"Funny how it used to seem like this huge city when I was young," he said. "Now it seems more like an overgrown small town."

"That's what I like about it. You can wrap your arms around it and become a part of it so easily."

"I didn't say I didn't like it. I like small towns. In fact, it's cities I hate."

She bit her tongue. If he was going to make everything into an argument, she just wouldn't talk anymore.

The silence stretched between them. She risked a quick look his way. His attention was on the other side of the river, giving her an opportunity to study him for a moment. He had a rugged, masculine appeal, untamed and proud of it. Pure Texas. She remembered he'd always looked so very good riding a horse.

But that was then. And remember, she'd never liked him much. She had to keep that in mind at all times.

Suddenly, as though there had been no pause in their conversation, he spoke softly.

"My mom brought me to San Antonio for a weekend one November when I was a kid, to see the Christmas lights on the river."

That surprised her, and not only because he was talking like a normal person for a change. "Just you? Not any of the others?" There were plenty of Allmans.

He shook his head. "Just me. I was about thirteen and she thought I needed something special. I think she was trying to make up for the fact that Pop was making it pretty plain that he considered Matt his fair-haired child and thought of me as good for nothing much."

He stopped, frowning fiercely. Why the hell was he telling her all this? Of all people, she was the last...

But maybe it was because they'd known each other forever, practically grown up side by side. Too bad he couldn't just think of her as a sister. But the feeling that swelled in him whenever he looked at her had nothing to do with brotherly love. So he had better stop looking.

"You were her favorite," she said softly.

"Me?" That startled him. When he thought of his mother, he remembered a warm smile and a feeling of peace. She was just about perfect in his book. No one could ever touch her. It still hurt to know she was gone. "Nah. She didn't have favorites. She was good to everyone."

Shelley nodded. "She was a wonderful woman and she died much too young." Reminders of that awful time, when Jodie's sweet mother was dying of complications from heart surgery, made her wince. "But believe me, she had a special soft spot for you."

He turned to look at her, frowning. "You were just a kid. You paid attention to things like that?"

She couldn't hold back a smile. "Of course."

His gaze lingered, then he turned away and her smile drooped.

But he'd unlocked a lot of memories. She'd spent so much time at that house, with that family, probably because she didn't have much of a family herself. All she had was her always busy single mother. No one else. Millie avoided any talk about who her father was, so she'd made one up for herself. Tall, handsome, kind and loving, he was ideal—though he tended to evaporate into mist whenever she tried to reach out to him. That was the trouble with fantasy fathers.

So that really didn't fill the lonely hole in her heart. She'd prayed every night for a brother or sister, until she'd finally gotten old enough to begin to understand why that wouldn't ever happen. So she'd attached herself to the Allmans.

"You seem to have grown up okay despite losing your mother," she told Rafe now. "And being left to the untender mercies of your father."

He shrugged. "Pop's okay."

That almost made her angry. It wasn't the way she remembered things.

"He can't hit you anymore, can he?" she said softly. "You're bigger than he is now."

He reacted as though she'd said something crazy.

"What? Ah come on, he never hit me all that much."

He turned to lean with his back against the railing, his arms crossed over his chest. This was something no one would ever understand. His father had always been rough on him. But that only made the times he came through and surprised the old man all the more satisfying.

"Anyway, that was the way his generation dealt with things. Say what you want about Pop, he's a man of his time."

She shook her head, wondering how he could defend the man. Jesse Allman was a character, a legend around their hometown of Chivaree, Texas. A hardscrabble sort of guy, he'd managed to work his much-scorned family out of poverty and up into dizzying success. He was a genius in his own way, and adept at turning his life around and making something of himself. But he hadn't been a gentle father.

"You wouldn't hit a child, would you?"

He gave her a look of weary resignation. "It's called spanking, Shelley. And no, I don't suppose I would do that. How about you?"

She shrugged. "I'm never going to have children."

He stared at her, then shook his head. "Going for that big career in the sky, are you?"

For some reason, she felt like shivering. Was she really considered a career woman now? Oh, well, she supposed that was better than some things she might be called.

"Something like that," she admitted reluctantly.

He turned back to look at the water. "You're doing pretty well. I've heard good things about your work from Clay in Legal."

Clay Branch, her supervisor in the legal division, another bothersome man in her life. "Maybe if I do a good job at this competition, Clay will finally pay some attention to my requests to get management training."

"You want to be a manager?"

"I want to move up in my field. And that's pretty much my only avenue, don't you think?"

"Maybe so." He grinned. "I guess that's why you're jumping at the chance to boss me around, huh?"

"I didn't set up the framework for this competition." She gazed at him challengingly. "But I'm not running from it, either. Do you feel threatened by that, Mr. Boss Man?"

Rafe didn't respond but he moved restlessly, indicating he was ready to walk on, and she obliged. They passed a small club. Pieces of acoustic guitar music floated out into the night. The crowd was thinning out and the lights were not quite so bright in this direction.

"You used to live here in San Antonio, didn't you?"

She nodded, feeling suddenly wary. It was not a period of her life she relished discussing. "Not for long," she murmured, looking away.

"And you worked for Jason McLaughlin during that time, didn't you?"

His question hit her like a slap in the face and she gasped softly. She sneaked a quick look at him. How much did he know?

Back in Chivaree, the McLaughlins were the family who founded and ran the town, and the Allmans were the outcasts. Things had changed over the last decade, and now the Allmans were riding high, running a company that was putting the McLaughlins into the shadows.

But the old legends still hung on. The McLaughlins were considered legitimate. The Allmans were the outlaws. And the two families had always hated each other.

So it was a big deal for Shelley, who had grown up identifying with the Allmans, to have worked for a McLaughlin. In many quarters, that would be considered the move of a traitor. Looking back, she considered it the move of a crazy person, a woman who had temporarily lost her mind and good sense. It certainly wasn't something she bragged about, or wanted to remember fondly.

"That was a long time ago," she said evasively.

"Only a little over a year, isn't it?" He stopped, hands shoved into his pockets and looked at her searchingly. "So I guess this will be a reunion of sorts for you."

Her heart was thumping in her chest and she reached up to finger her gold necklace nervously. "What are you talking about?"

"I just noticed it on the roster. McLaughlin Management is in the competition." His stare was hard and penetrating. "Jason is here. Didn't you know?"

"No, I didn't know." She wanted to reach out for something to lean on but she knew she couldn't allow herself that luxury. This was something she hadn't prepared for. She knew Jason's business was doing very well, but they had never entered the competition before. Why did they have to decide to start now?

"Or is that exactly why you asked to be included in the team even though you had your turn last year?"

She looked into his face, bewildered. Did he really think she wanted a chance to get close to Jason McLaughlin again?

Then he knew—or at least suspected—about her past relationship with the man. That was embarrassing.

Still, a lot of people knew, so why wouldn't he? It wasn't anything she was proud of. And she certainly didn't yearn for a repeat performance, if that was what he was implying. Anger shivered through her.

"Don't worry, Rafe. I won't be taking time off from the competition to dally with our competitors. We'll put up a good fight for your beloved trophy."

She started to stomp off but he grabbed her arm and pulled her back.

"Shelley, don't act like I'm all alone in this. Of all people, you should understand. We both come from dirt-poor backgrounds. We know what it's like to scramble for a little dignity."

She turned her face away, unwilling to join him in this, even rhetorically, as he went on.

"We're not like the McLaughlins, either one of us. No silver spoons for us. We fight for every inch. So I think you understand me when I say we've got to win this thing. And a good part of the satisfaction in that will be beating the McLaughlins."

"Beating the McLaughlins," she echoed softly.

"Sure. They've always got the establishment behind them. We're the little guy. We have to try harder."

That was Rafe to a T—always trying harder. Always trying to show his father that he could be good at things. And the funny thing was, he was very good at just about everything. Too bad Jesse Allman never seemed to notice.

But she didn't want to waste her time feeling empathy for Rafe. He was studying her reaction and she knew it. He wanted to know that she was on the side of Allman Industries, that she wasn't going to defect to the enemy. Rebelliously she refused to give him that comfort.

She looked out at the water again. "I thought maybe, now that Jodie is marrying Kurt McLaughlin, the feud between your two families would begin to fade away."

His mouth hardened. "The feud will begin to fade away when the McLaughlins stop being coldhearted bastards. Except for Kurt, of course. He's always been different from the rest of them."

She nodded. She had to agree on that score. Kurt had started working at Allman Industries some months before, despite a lot of resistance and bitterness from his own family. And when Jodie had come home to work there, too, a romance between the two of them had quickly blossomed.

Shelley loved Jodie and wished her the best, but she had to admit she was a little worried at first about the McLaughlin angle to it all. Her own experience told her

that all the years of antagonism between the two families was based on more than pure spite.

She was still thinking about the McLaughlins as they
started to walk back toward the hotel. There had been a
time when she'd been so in love with Jason McLaughlin
she could hardly see straight. And maybe that was why
she didn't realize what a jerk he was until it was too late.

No. Wait. That wasn't really fair.

Jason hadn't been so much a jerk as she herself had
been blind and hopelessly naive. She hadn't known he
was married at first. From what she learned later, the
marriage was stormy—with the two of them separated
more often than they were together. She had started dating Jason during one of those separations. Still, only a
fool would have believed his lies about it being over for
good. Anyone with half a brain should have seen where
things were headed. Only, she had been too over-
whelmed by the chance to be with Jason. She *had* a
brain, she just hadn't used it. She still cringed when she
remembered the day his wife had returned to find Shelley ensconced in their apartment. The bitter contempt
in the woman's eyes had been like a brand on her soul.
And she knew she deserved every bit of that scorn.

"So I know you're going to cooperate here. Right?"

He wanted reassurance. Well, too bad. At this point
she wasn't sure he deserved it. Looking at him, she
made a face.

"Are you still obsessed with being number one all the
time, Rafe? Is that all life is to you, always winning?"

"What's wrong with winning? It's better than being a loser." His dark gaze raked over her sardonically. "Or maybe you prefer losers?"

"Not really. I'd say I prefer people of goodwill."

He started to say something, then stopped himself and shook his head. "Goodwill, huh? Hey, I'm dripping with it."

"Really?" The picture that conjured up almost made her laugh. She raised her eyebrows instead, then smiled faintly and made a grand gesture with her hand. "Perhaps I should clarify. I prefer people with a broader scope," she said, purposefully making it sound snooty.

"Oh." She was happy to see amusement begin to bubble in his gaze. "Broad scope, eh? Excuse me while I adjust my cravat."

She gestured again, chin in the air. "You're excused. Carry on."

"Such graciousness. You put me to shame."

She smiled impishly. "Then my work here is done."

A faint grin actually appeared on his face. "Oh, no, honey. I'm going to be more of a challenge than you can imagine."

Her breath caught in a little hiccup in her throat and she blinked to cover it up. "That's a little scary. I can imagine a lot." She flashed him a look. "I'll clarify even further. I prefer men with a little sophistication."

He cocked an eyebrow. "I suppose what you really prefer is Jason McLaughlin."

Her head whipped around and she glared at him. To her complete shock, he actually looked chagrined.

"Sorry," he muttered. "That was a low blow."

"You should know," she said tartly. "You're the king."

"Of low blows?"

"And other assorted indignities."

"Indignities." He mocked the way she'd said the word, humor softening the edges. "Gettin' sorta high falutin with your language there, girl. I knew you way back when we were both prairie rats. You can't fool me."

He was teasing her, but in a gentle way, not the way he used to when they were young. If he didn't watch out, she was going to start to like him.

"Maybe you can't be fooled," she said. "But at the same time, you *can* be persuaded. You're a smart guy. You know there's nothing wrong with reaching for something a little higher."

A boisterous bunch of young people was headed straight for them. Reaching out, he put a hand at the nape of her neck, guiding her with a protective touch as the youngsters passed.

"Just as long as you don't forget where you came from," he murmured.

The feel of his hand on her skin was seductive and she felt a lazy sense of warmth seeping into her system. Taking a quick step to the side, she managed to pull away as she pretended to need the room to turn and face him.

"Well, look at you," she said earnestly. "You were in

a business suit this afternoon. You had on a tie and everything. Your shirt was crisp and white and your slacks had a great crease. You looked wonderful. Your father never looked like that in his life."

His face twisted into a thoughtful frown. "So I'm aiming for a higher place just like you think I oughta, just by wearing a suit?" He gave her a look of pure exasperation. "Listen, Shelley. Nobody ever worked harder to make a 'higher place' in this world than my father did."

"Except maybe my mother," she shot back. "How do you think she managed to run Millie's Café on her own? Nobody handed her anything."

A reluctant grin began to surface again on his handsome face. "Well…my pop can outhustle your mom."

Her chin went out. "Cannot."

His eyes twinkled. "Can, too."

She smiled back, just barely, flashing her eyes at him. "Well…maybe. But he can't cook like she can."

He nodded. "You got me there."

They were back in front of the hotel. Without saying a word, they both paused. Neither seemed anxious to go in. She turned to look at him and he met her gaze.

"So you swear you didn't come to the conference because of McLaughlin?" he demanded.

She hesitated, then held up her hand like a Girl Scout. "I swear to you. I probably wouldn't have come myself if I'd known he was going to be here."

He nodded slowly as though thinking that over. "So

tell me…why did you come? Just what is your ulterior motive?"

She couldn't keep meeting his gaze after that. Because the truth was, "ulterior motive" was a good phrase for her purpose. She had agreed to come at the last minute, knowing it would give her an opportunity she wouldn't otherwise have to do a little detective work that needed to be done. But she couldn't tell Rafe about that. To do so would involve telling a secret that wasn't hers to share.

Taking in a deep breath, she raised her gaze to his again. "You know, there are some things that are just plain private," she said firmly, though her pulse gave a nervous flutter as she noted his reaction. "My reasons have nothing to do with the business," she added. "And anyway, you have no right to ask me."

"You won't tell me." He looked astonished at her defiance.

She shook her head and shrugged, her palms out. "You have no need to know." It was only the truth. Why couldn't he accept it and move on?

His eyes looked very dark in the lamplight. "You realize that means I can't put my suspicions to rest."

She turned her head so fast her long silky hair whipped around her shoulders. He was being impossible. But then, that was his nature, wasn't it? She'd almost forgotten with him seeming so approachable.

"Then you just suspect away all you want, honey," she told him with her thickest Texas drawl. "As long as you do a good job for me tomorrow. Because for the time being, I…am…the…boss." With a look daring him to dispute what she'd said, she whirled and strode for the elevators.

Chapter Three

In the morning, the first person Shelley saw as she stepped off the elevator on the lobby floor was the very man she dreaded seeing—Jason McLaughlin.

"Shelley. It's been a long time." The tall blue-eyed man in the Italian silk suit stepped forward and took both her hands in his, smiling down at her. "You look wonderful."

For a moment she wasn't sure if she was going to be able to speak. Did he know her well enough to see the turmoil her heart was in? Did he notice the tightness around her mouth, the panic in her eyes?

Probably not. After all, there was no real evidence that he had ever known much of anything about her, that he had ever really cared. She'd warmed his bed and kept his apartment picked up. That was all he'd ever really wanted, wasn't it?

On the other hand, she'd spent all of her teenage years watching everything he ever did. She'd even kept a notebook about him, hidden under her mattress and only brought out late at night to write some new secret in. *Saw Jason at the feed store this afternoon. He had holes in his jeans and looked so cool. He turned my way and I almost had a heart attack. But he walked right by. I don't think he saw me.*

He was her one and only teenage crush, and when she moved to San Antonio after college and got a job in his firm, she was in seventh heaven. And then he actually noticed her, picked her out to be his special assistant, and very quickly, his special girl. It was like a dream come true. Until she woke up.

"Jason," she said, finding her voice at last. "I'm surprised to find you here. I would have thought this would be a bit too bourgeois for you."

"Don't be silly," he said, beaming at her. "This conference has become the highlight of the business year in San Antonio. We came to win the competition." He laughed lightly, his white teeth flashing

Sharks have white teeth, too, she thought a bit wildly. *Translation: beware!*

Aloud she said, "Good luck. We're hoping for a good result as well." But she felt as though she were in deep water and in danger of losing her grip on the surface with predators circling.

He still had hold of one of her hands and he tried to tug her a bit closer. Looking down dreamily into her eyes in a way that would once have sent her reeling, he said coaxingly, "Listen, we're both on our way to breakfast, aren't we? Come have it with me. We'll get a booth. We need to catch up on old times."

She opened her mouth to respond, planning to put him in his place with a well-chosen word or two. But she wasn't quick enough, because suddenly Rafe was there, sliding his arm around her shoulders.

"Sorry, McLaughlin," he said coolly. "I've already got her booked up. You're out of luck."

"Rafe." Jason's face changed completely, but only for a moment. Very quickly he had his smooth, cultured mask on again. "I would make a crack about bad pennies, but that would be rude."

"Go ahead and be as rude as you like," Rafe told him evenly. "We're all such old friends. You can be yourself around us if you like."

Jason had a faint smile that didn't warm his eyes at all. "Have a nice day," he said, sarcasm coloring his tone as he turned away.

"We will," Rafe promised, tightening his hold on Shelley's shoulders as he began to lead her toward the breakfast area.

She went willingly enough, but her nerves were jangling and she pushed his arm away. The hostess indicated a table big enough to take the others as they arrived. Shelley turned and faced Rafe as they approached it.

"I could have handled that myself, you know," she said.

"I have no doubt about it," he said smoothly, escorting her into her seat at the table. "If you'd wanted to."

Her eyes widened. He really didn't trust her. She leaned forward, looking at him across the table. "Are you accusing me of something here?" she demanded.

He smiled thinly, then picked up the huge menu and began to peruse it. "I'm not going to tolerate any traitors on our team," he said from behind it. "Just giving you fair warning."

"Rafe Allman…." She clenched her hands into fists on the table. "You…you make me so mad!"

He looked around the menu as though surprised. "No reason for anger, Shelley. Don't you get it?"

He dropped the menu and reached out to grab one of her hands. "The fact that we strike sparks off each other should be a plus for us. It's great for creativity. It produces a tension that can help us create a dynamic that will blow everyone else in this competition away."

She blinked at him. "Either that, or we'll kill each other."

He nodded. "That's always a possibility, of course."

But his eyes were smiling and she couldn't resist smiling back for just a moment. Then she pulled her hand away from his and reached for her own menu.

"Don't bother," he said. "I know what I'm ordering for you."

"What?"

"Dollar-size blueberry pancakes with cherry syrup and sausages."

She stared at him, dumbfounded. He looked up at her, and she almost thought he was half embarrassed.

"Listen, I remember how you used to pack it away on Saturday mornings when Rita would cook a big breakfast for us all."

Rita was the big sister, the oldest daughter in the Allman clan. "She cooked enough for half the neighborhood it seemed sometimes," she murmured, remembering.

He nodded. "Anyway, you always loved those little round pancakes and that thick cherry syrup."

How funny that he remembered that. A wave of nostalgia swept over her and she smiled. "Those were the days before I had to start watching my figure."

"Hey, I'll watch your figure for you. No problem at all. And I'll let you know if I notice anything going wrong with it."

She sighed. "Now you're starting to disappoint me. That is such a lame joke."

"Who's joking?" He said it softly, his eyes burning.

The waitress arrived at their table, pouring them both cups of steaming coffee, and Rafe ordered for them. Shelley was too involved in thinking over what he'd just said and the way he'd looked to remember that she'd planned to stop him from ordering pancakes for her. And then it was too late and she decided to let it go.

She looked at him a bit warily. He looked back. She searched for something to say.

"Well. Ready for the big day?"

He grunted and took a sip of scalding coffee, making a face as it burned his tongue.

"The workshops last until noon," she said, talking quickly to fill the silence. "We'll meet for lunch in the Tapa Grill and then our group will adjourn to my room to decide on our plan. I've got some really interesting ideas."

"Do you?" He looked surprised.

"Yes, I do."

He shrugged. "I've got a few ideas of my own. Some pretty great ideas. I guess it will be the battle of the ideas. We'll see whose ideas come out on top."

She made a face. He was making this sound like some sort of monster truck rally or something. "I think mine are pretty good."

He nodded, his dark gaze searching her face. "'Pretty good'," he echoed mockingly. "You see, there's your problem, Shelley, 'Pretty good' is not going to win this competition. 'Over-the-top pretty damn sensational' might have a chance." He shook his head, stabbing a fork into the air. "This is what worries me. You don't have the killer instinct."

She wrinkled her nose. "I should hope not."

"But don't you get it? The killer instinct is going to be bottom-line imperative to win this."

"Oh, stop being so melodramatic. We're going to do just fine."

He stared at her for a moment, then groaned, throwing his head back. "Shelley, Shelley, Shelley. You've got to toughen up, girl. You cringe at the sight of blood. Metaphorically speaking. You can't go for the throat, regardless. You're not ready, willing and able to wage all-out war on everyone and everything that gets in your way." His penetrating gaze stung. "And I am." He sat back, looking infuriatingly pleased with himself. "You'd better leave this to me."

She had to bite her tongue for a moment, and even count to ten. She didn't want to start screeching at him. That would be embarrassing, especially with Jason McLaughlin sitting across the room, watching every move they made.

"You go ahead and give advice to the B group," she said at last. "You *are* the highest ranking officer from Allman Industries. You have a right to manage us all you want. But as for our group, for the next four days, I'm the boss. You're going to do what I say, Rafe Allman."

He looked at her with heavily lidded eyes. "Is this some kind of payback?"

"Payback!" She rolled her eyes. "You are such an infuriating man. You really think it's all about you, don't you?"

"Well, isn't it?"

She stared at him for a long moment. He really meant it.

"You know, you're right. This is payback." She leaned forward again, speaking earnestly. "It's payback for the time you put green food coloring in the shampoo while Jodie and I were swimming and we ended up with green hair—and green faces and green hands."

His eyebrows knit together as he recalled the incident. "I must admit, I hadn't thought that through very well when I did it." Still, he grinned. "But you two sure did look funny."

She wasn't going to concede that. She wasn't going to concede anything to him anymore.

"It's also payback for the time I was drinking milk at your house and thought I felt a lump go down and you convinced me you'd put a frog in my glass. I nearly went crazy, sure that I could feel it wiggle around inside me."

"Poor little frog." He actually looked concerned, glancing at what he could see of her tummy area. "He must be in there still."

She gaped at him. "There was no frog!"

He looked doubtful. "You'll never know for sure, will you?"

How many years did you get for murder in Texas these days? Surely jurors would take into account that this was a crime of passion. Passionate anger!

She'd started down a memory lane that didn't seem to have an end. Now that she'd brought it up, she could think of so many times he'd driven her crazy.

"How about when I was just learning to drive and you told me the bump I went over was Jodie's dog Buster. I couldn't find that dog anywhere for hours, crying the whole time, thinking he was in the bushes somewhere, hurt."

He grimaced. "That one might have been a little mean."

"A little!" She shook her head, glaring at him. "I hated you!"

"For what? I was just being a dopey kid. And so were you." He looked at her quizzically. "Remember the time you switched the tuna sandwich in my lunch bag with one made of cat food?"

"I didn't do that." She managed to look innocent. "And anyway, it was Jodie's idea."

He grinned and she couldn't help but smile back, just a little. But there wasn't time for anything else. Jim and Jaye were coming toward their table and some of the others weren't far behind. Shelley sat up a little taller and put on her more public smile. Too much dallying with Rafe Allman was a danger to her peace of mind, and probably to her sanity. The day was going to be very full and it was time to get her head on straight.

An hour later, Shelley was sneaking down the back stairway to the parking garage, hoping no one had noticed her slipping out of the time management workshop. Skipping that and the forum on brainstorming would give her exactly two hours before she had to be back for lunch. Hopefully, she would have some answers to her questions by then.

Her car was waiting and soon she was cruising along the familiar streets of San Antonio, heading for Chuy's Café. She really hoped this top-secret mission she was on for Rafe's older brother, Matt, would be successful.

She'd always looked on Matt as her own older brother as well. He was the sort of guy you could depend on, the sort you wanted only good things to happen to. She'd been in college in Dallas while he was going to med school there and she'd become good friends with his girlfriend at the time, Penny Hagar. She and Penny had even shared an apartment for a while. So her relationship with Matt had only become stronger. And when he'd come to her a few days ago and explained that he needed to find Penny again, Shelley had jumped at the chance to help him out.

Now she was on her way to the coffee shop that had served as a hangout of sorts for the group of young people she had socialized with when she'd lived here in San Antonio. Hopefully someone would remember Penny, who had supposedly returned to San Antonio after leaving Dallas three years before.

She knew Penny had a brother named Quinn who was still in the area. In fact, she had hung around with a group of people who knew Quinn when she'd lived here. He was more or less on the periphery of the group, but they'd been friendly acquaintances and had even talked about Penny a time or two. If she could only find Quinn, Penny's whereabouts ought to be easy to locate.

A little over an hour later, she was turning back into the hotel parking area. She'd found a couple of old acquaintances having a late breakfast at Chuy's. They had been very helpful in giving her names and telephone numbers that might serve as leads, but she really hadn't gotten hold of any firm information that would help her search.

Still, she was back in time to stop by her room for a moment to freshen up before she needed to meet the others for lunch. Once again, she took the back way, hoping to avoid anyone she knew. Taking out her card, she slid it quickly into the slot in her door and went inside, sighing with relief that she'd made it without being observed. She switched on the light in the entryway and walked into the semidarkened room when a voice stopped her cold.

"Welcome back, Shelley."

Rafe! She whirled and faced him where he sat in the large armchair by the window. Putting a hand over her heart, she caught her breath. "How did you get in here?" she demanded.

He shrugged, his face in shadows. "What can I say? Maids love me."

"Oh!"

She walked quickly to the drapes and pulled them open, flooding the room with light, then turned to face him again.

"So where've you been?" he asked.

"Out."

"So I noticed." His hard mouth twisted. "Out where?"

She turned away and he went on.

"I've been thinking this over. I let you outmaneuver me last night and that's not going to happen again."

Rising, he stood where she couldn't avoid him. "I was under the impression that I was the boss, as it were. *Your* boss, at the very least. And as such, I think I can demand a few answers from you. Don't give me that old excuse about this being none of my business. You're here on company time." His look hardened. "So I'm going to ask you once again. Where have you been?"

She looked up into his dark eyes. "Driving around," she said reluctantly.

"Driving around where?"

She shrugged. "Different areas of San Antonio."

One dark eyebrow rose. "Just seeing the sights?"

She looked away.

"What were you looking for, Shelley?"

Closing her eyes, she bit her lip. If only she could tell him. But she couldn't betray Matt that way. Opening her eyes again, she looked at him beseechingly. "Oh, Rafe, please don't ask. I really can't tell you that."

He stared at her for a long moment, then turned away, looking out the picture window at the blue sky. "You weren't just thinking?" he offered her. "Mulling over your life?"

She knew he was giving her a way out, if she wanted it, and her heart skipped. She wouldn't have expected that from him. Too bad she couldn't make things easier for both of them and accept his offer.

"No," she said softly, shaking her head. "I'm not going to lie to you."

Turning slowly, he faced her again. "It just so happened that Jason McLaughlin was missing from his workshop, too."

"Oh, for heaven's sake, you don't think that I was out meeting with Jason, do you?"

"I don't want to think that."

She threw up her hands and he caught them with his. "No, actually I think you're too smart for that. But you've got to admit, it looks pretty fishy."

It did. She knew that. Suddenly her eyes were misting. Everything seemed so relentlessly difficult. No matter which way she turned she was bound to hurt someone. Maybe even herself. Despite all that, a smile trembled on her lips as she looked up at him. His face softened and he pulled her closer.

"God, Shelley," he said, his voice low and husky. "Why'd you have to turn out so damn beautiful?"

She drew in a shaky breath and smiled almost impishly. "To annoy you, I guess. There doesn't seem to be much else it's good for."

He hesitated, his gaze searching hers, and then he kissed her.

His unexpected embrace sent shock waves through her. She'd been kissed before and by some pretty great guys, but there was nobody like Rafe when it came to kissing. This was just like that New Year's Eve had been, only more so. His mouth was filled with a sort of irresistible heat that made her yearn toward him, hungry for more. His tongue scraping against hers set off a series of small explosions in her nervous system, making her think of naked bodies rolling together on satin sheets. The man had a magic. That couldn't be denied. And when he drew back, swearing softly and shaking his head as though he couldn't believe he'd just done that, she had to fight hard to keep from whimpering for more.

Chapter Four

He should never have kissed her.

Rafe stared at the chart Candy Yang had put up to show them when their presentation was scheduled but his mind was on Shelley's mouth. Here he was in the middle of a business meeting in her hotel room, doing important work, and all he could think about was kissing her again.

Well, Shelley obviously didn't share the sentiment. She couldn't get rid of him fast enough after the deed was done. She'd blown their embrace off as if it had never happened and he had played along to preserve his healthy male pride.

This was stupid and it wasn't like him. He knew how to focus. He knew what was important. Kissing Shelley was not important, dammit!

It was just about time for him to give his proposal for the plan for their entry. It was a winner and he had no doubt they could sweep the competition if they played it right. The strategy had some real meat to it.

Shelley had already given her presentation and he felt a little sorry for her. Her idea involved day care or something. How had she put it?

"A human resources goal of setting up job sharing arrangements for employees who have children to avoid losing some of their best employees."

He wasn't really listening as she gave her talk. For one thing, the subject didn't exactly excite him. For another, he was obsessing on her mouth and the way it formed words rather than the words it was forming.

What did they call that…bee-stung lips? He grimaced. He didn't like that. This had nothing to do with insects, but everything to do with the fact that he wanted to kiss her so badly it was like an undercurrent in his blood.

Anyway, he'd almost wished he'd told her not to bother with presenting her idea. Everyone was asking her questions about it, taking up a lot of time. But he was sure that once they heard his brilliant proposition, hers would be forgotten.

He glanced at his watch. Who knew, maybe they could wrap this up quickly, get rid of the other people in the room, and have a little time together before the afternoon session began. Involuntarily, he glanced at the bed in the standard hotel room model. He had a flash

of two bodies intertwined tangling those crisp white
sheets and couldn't help but smile slightly.

When he looked up, his gaze met Shelley's. And suddenly he was blushing again. He swore softly. This was
getting to be ridiculous. It was as though being around
her catapulted him back into his teenage years. Only
when he was a teenager, he wouldn't have been caught
dead being attracted to Shelley Sinclair.

Maybe that was the secret antidote. Maybe if he cast
his mind into rewind and recalled what she was like when
he couldn't stand her, he could get his mind straight again.

Squinting, he thought back to that last summer before she went away to college. The picture his mind
dredged up was funny at first. He remembered Shelley
at the Fourth of July picnic. She'd worn the prettiest little sundress, her hair all curled and nicely coiffed, but
then someone pushed her off the dock into the lake and
she came up sputtering, looking like a drowned rat.

His mouth tilted in a slight smile as he thought of it.
Yeah, everyone had laughed their heads off over that
one. He'd laughed right along with them. Only, then, as
the water molded that little sundress to her body, he'd
begun to see something not quite so laughable. That was
the first time he'd really noticed how large and full her
breasts had become, the way her waist nipped in, emphasizing the full rounded nature of her hips. Shelley had turned into a very attractively proportioned
woman while he was still thinking of her as a snot-
nosed brat.

"Rafe?"

"What?" He looked up, getting the guilty feeling familiar from being called on unexpectedly in class.

"Didn't you have a suggestion for the contest?"

"Oh. Yeah, sure."

He rose and turned to the group. He knew them all, most of them pretty darn well, and he was sure they were going to like this one. Standing before them with his hands shoved into his pockets, he launched into his sales pitch.

"I'm counting on your discretion," he told them, looking squarely into each gaze in turn. "This is information I just got today. It won't be announced until Monday. But Quarter Season Ranch is going up for sale."

Mouths dropped all around the room and he watched with quiet satisfaction. Quarter Season Ranch was one of the oldest and largest in their area and no one had thought that old cowboy Jake Quartermain would ever let go of it. The guy had to be in his nineties. Now it seemed his grandchildren had prevailed upon him and he was finally selling out.

"But, what exactly does this mean for us?" Candy asked, bright-eyed.

Rafe smiled, giving a dramatic pause, and then he told them. It meant work. It meant lobbying to make sure the zoning went their way. It meant creating designs for land use. It meant a full court press of Allman Industries to beat their competitors out for that ranch. Just think of the vineyards they would have. The place was perfect in setting and soil composition. All that had ever been on it before were cows.

"You're going to have a fight on your hands," Jerry Perez, the plant manager, said skeptically. "There will be big developers salivating for that land."

"That's why we'll have to move fast and get the ear of a few legislators to make sure the zoning goes our way," Rafe said with satisfaction. "I've already spent a few hours on the phone with some Austin people. But here's the part that's relevant to you at the moment. Putting our heads together and producing the game plan for that fight will be our entry in the contest."

He grinned, shrugging. "Smooth, huh? We have to do this foundational stuff anyway. On Monday morning, when you all show up at work, we'll have it halfway there."

He went on to explain. He was excited about it and he could tell he was communicating that excitement. People were nodding. He had them in the palm of his hand. It was great, really, a stroke of genius.

When he was finished, he looked expectantly at them all.

"What do you think?" he asked confidently.

There was an uncomfortable silence for a long moment.

"It sounds great, Rafe, but…" Candy looked uncertain. "I guess we'd better vote on it."

"Vote?" He shrugged. He supposed that would make it official. "Why not? Everyone who's for my plan, raise your hand."

"Wait!" Candy looked toward Shelley. "Don't you think it ought to be a secret ballot?"

Shelley rose slowly from her seat. Her face was flushed as though she were upset about something and he couldn't imagine what it could be.

"Yes," she said clearly, giving him a look that had a little too much defiance built into it for his taste. "A secret ballot is just the thing."

It was a waste of time, but he sighed and nodded. "Okay. Let's get it over with."

It couldn't be that easy, of course. First someone had to find a pad with enough papers on it, then the right amount of pencils had to be produced and then Shelley insisted on a quick summary of both plans to remind everyone what was involved.

"My plan deals with the problem every parent has as an employee—what to do about child care, especially for the youngest ones, the sick ones, the ones who need after school care. In this scenario, our workplace sets up a child-care area where employees can bring their kids and each person who uses the service donates a certain amount of time as a child-care provider. It's work sharing. The company hires a supervisor to coordinate things and throws in some extra time off for employees who participate."

She then did a quick rundown on Rafe's plan, emphasizing its benefits in a way he couldn't complain about. He was satisfied. But he was looking at his watch by the time they settled down and voted. He wrote out his own plan's name quickly, folded the paper and handed it to Candy. Then he went to sit down in a place that would give him the best view of Shelley's lips.

She looked up and caught him in the act. He smiled at her, determined never again to be disconcerted by letting her see he was attracted to her.

She didn't smile back. Holding up the papers, she said calmly, "Thank you all for participating. My plan has won. I've drawn up a script and made lists for each of you. Pick up your copy on your way out. It is getting late and the afternoon lecture begins in half an hour, so if you have any questions…"

Rafe blinked, incredulous.

"Wait a minute," he said. "What do you mean, your plan won?"

She licked those beautiful lips and met his outraged gaze. "I got more votes, Rafe."

He almost choked. "I don't believe you. Let's see them."

It was her turn to redden. "I got more votes. Leave it at that."

"That can't be." He really thought there had to be some mistake. "My plan's perfect."

The others were shuffling their feet and not meeting his gaze. He began to realize things really weren't going to work out the way he'd thought they should.

"Your plan is a very good one," Shelley conceded. "But my plan won."

He narrowed his eyes. Was that a spark of triumph he saw in her eyes? "What was the vote?" he demanded.

"Rafe, just…"

"I want to know. What was the vote?"

Shelley drew a deep breath. "Six to one," she said softly.

He thought he hadn't heard her correctly for a second or two, then he realized he'd had a pure and simple mutiny on his hands. He looked at the others in the room with an outraged sense of betrayal.

"No," he said shaking his head. "You can't possibly be for hers over mine. That just defies logic."

Candy finally looked up and tried to smile.

"Look, Rafe, there's no question your idea shows potential to appreciate earnings and all that good stuff. And if we were back home and the outcome mattered to our bottom line—we'd have to go with it."

She looked around the room for support and the others nodded.

"But that's not what we're doing here. We were all discussing this earlier, before you came. We're presenting something to judges. Only half of them will be from the actual business world. The rest include a local TV anchor person, a magazine writer and the head of the local garden club."

Candy looked at him earnestly. "These are touchy-feely people. They're not going to care about the bottom line. They want something that plays on the heartstrings. The child care exchange idea will be right up that particular alley."

Rafe looked at them all, then at Shelley. He was angry. He was affronted. He even felt a bit betrayed. And he knew this wouldn't have happened if Shelley hadn't taken over as boss the way she had—taken to it with a vengeance. He wanted to lash out at them all and tell them what he thought of them.

But he wasn't stupid and he knew having a tantrum about it would be foolish. It wouldn't get him anywhere and it would make him look like a sore loser. Was he a sore loser? Hell yes!

But he calmed down. This wasn't the end. After all, there was more than one way to bell a cat. So, exerting all the self-discipline he could muster, he shrugged and smiled at them all.

"Okay," he said. "What do you want me to do?"

Shelley raised a finely sculpted eyebrow and looked at him sideways. She wasn't fooled. She knew he hadn't given up.

"I'm going to ask Candy to take a couple of people with her, along with a video camera, and do a little taping for background footage," she said. "I've already called the director at a private school nearby and they said they would allow it."

"Okay," he said. "But what's my role in all this?"

Before she had a chance to say anything to him, her cell phone rang and she excused herself, retreating to the little table by the window while the rest of them rose, reached for assignment papers and began to talk excitedly among themselves.

Rafe smiled and answered when spoken to, but his attention was absorbed by Shelley and her phone call.

Concentrating hard, he was able to make out a few phrases here and there.

"Thanks so much for the information," he heard just below the buzz of conversation as she prepared to hang up. "I'll get over there as soon as I can."

She turned to look at him as she put the phone away. He held her gaze, but this time he didn't smile.

Shelley knew she ought to be feeling good right now. She ought to be pumping her fist in the air and bowing to the accolades of the crowd. After all, she'd defeated the great Rafe Allman in a vote.

She hadn't been sure how it would go, and actually, she'd been surprised it had gone so decisively her way. Everyone loved her idea. All except Rafe, who hadn't been paying attention when she presented it anyway. But the others voted with her and that gave her a feeling of empowerment like she hadn't had in a long, long time. Maybe she was actually doing something right for a change.

But then there was Rafe—and the feeling of triumph hadn't lasted. She didn't like to see anyone lose when you came right down to it. Even if it was Rafe Allman. She knew he felt as though the rug had been pulled out from under him. And she knew him well enough to know he would have something else up his sleeve. He didn't give up this easily. She was going to have to be careful.

Still, all in all, it had gone really well. She was doing

better than she'd expected in holding her own against his overpowering presence on her team.

Well, except for that slipup earlier when they'd melted into a kiss. But that was a one-time deal. She'd obsess over that later. Right now she had to get away and try an address an old friend had phoned her with. She only had a short time to find Quinn so she had to take every opportunity.

She slipped out of the lecture by the back way, hurrying down the hall, hoping to avoid being seen and feeling like a criminal. But what the heck—these lectures pretty much contained common sense. That was something she had in spades.

She used her cell phone to call for her car to be ready at the front entrance as she made her way around the building. And there it was, right on time. She handed the attendant a bill and slipped into the driver's seat, not realizing she had company until the attendant had firmly closed her door.

"Rafe Allman!" she cried in dismay as she turned toward the man who was filling her passenger's seat. "Get out of this car!"

There he sat, big as life, and he had the gall to look surprised at her reaction. "Why?"

She bit her lip to keep herself from screaming, then raised an imploring hand and waved it at him. "Because you should be at the afternoon session."

He pretended bewilderment at her statement. "If you can miss it, why can't I?"

"Oh!" She closed her eyes for a moment, holding back fury. "I have something I just have to do. I'll be back as quickly as possible. In no time at all." She looked at him and tried to keep from letting her anger get out of hand. "But someone has to be there to make sure they get to work on things. Listen, you go on into the hotel and…"

He grinned. "Nice try, Shell. But it won't wash. You're the boss, remember? It's your idea we're supposed to be working on. You're the indispensable one, not me."

Clenching her jaw, she glared at him. "Is that what this is all about? You're upset because you lost the vote and you're going to take it out on me?"

"No."

He frowned, having second thoughts about his protestation of innocence.

"Well, I *am* upset that I lost. My proposal is a very good one. Something like that doesn't fall into your lap every day. I have the inside track on something that is going to be common knowledge next week and I think we really should take advantage of it."

He cocked an eyebrow her way, sure she must understand that he was right. Any clear-thinking person could see that. Unless their view was clouded by private animosity and petulance.

"Too bad," she said crisply.

"Come on, Shelley. You know my idea would work better. It's based on something solid and substantial, not fluff."

She drew in a deep breath, staring at him. She would not give in to temptation and lunge at his throat. Staying calm would win in the long run.

Think Zen. Think peace.

"And the truth is," he added, "I think the day-care thing is a lousy idea."

"But mysteriously popular," she pointed out carefully, marveling at her own self-control.

He nodded. "Very mysteriously." He made a face, then looked at her sharply. "But that is not the matter at hand."

She blinked. "No?"

"No. The matter at hand is—where the hell are you going?"

Nowhere if she couldn't get rid of him.

She stared at her own hands on the wheel of the car, trying for the stone-faced look. "It's none of your business."

"It may not be any of my business, but I'm not getting out of the car, so I guess I'll find out soon enough."

Turning toward him, she felt suddenly drained. Staying firm wasn't working. Saying mean things wasn't working. Beating him in the vote hadn't even chastened him. What hadn't she tried? Pleading for mercy?

Taking a deep breath, she went into pleading mode. "Oh, Rafe, please…"

That was as far as she got before a horn honked from behind them. Rafe turned to look and waved an acknowledgment to the attendant.

"Well darn it all," he said with a smug glance her way.

"Looks like we're going to have to take off. They want you to move out of the way. You're causing congestion."

"And you're causing *indi*gestion," she quipped through gritted teeth as she started the engine and began edging down the driveway.

"Sorry. That's what happens to people who try to sneak around behind other people's backs and…"

She couldn't stand any more of this. Heading for the main street, she gave up on trying to keep everything from him. It had become an untenable position anyway. But she talked without looking at him.

"Okay, look. I'll tell you basically what I'm doing. If you promise to go back to the hotel."

"No promises, Shelley. I'm here for the duration."

"Oh!"

"Calm down. You're driving. I'm just coming along for the ride." He looked over at her. "But you might as well give me some idea of what you're up to anyway."

She took a deep breath and let it out slowly. There didn't seem to be any point any longer in keeping everything a secret. Maybe she could foster some goodwill on his part if she let him in on some of it. She might as well try. He was probably going to figure out this much for himself anyway.

"Okay," she said reluctantly. "Here's the deal. I'm trying to find a man named Quinn Hagar."

He went very still. "An old boyfriend?" he asked softly.

"Hardly." She rolled her eyes. "It's nothing like that.

I just need…to get some information from him. For someone else."

"Who?"

She glanced at him. "I can't tell you that. We've been over this ground before."

"So it's someone I know." He looked at her sharply. "It has to be, or you would tell me who it was."

She sighed. The man was impossible. Making a turn, she began to head toward the seedy side of town.

Rafe went on speculating. "Okay, you've said it's not McLaughlin."

"It's not him."

"Hmm. Is it—?"

"Don't start this game, Rafe," she cut in firmly. "I'm not going to play."

He nodded. "That's smart of you, actually. I had a long list ready to quiz you on. That would have been somewhat tedious."

She shook her head as she slowed to a stop at a light and looked toward the heavens. "Why are you torturing me?"

"Why not?" He grinned. "Who better to torture than you, my lifelong nemesis."

She looked at him, wondering how they had come to this stage in their relationship. It seemed so strange. She'd known Rafe Allman all her life, and yet she didn't really know this man beside her. Was he a good guy, after all?

He certainly came from a good family. Well, his

mother had been an angel. His father was a bit more problematic. Still, his sister Jodie was a peach and her best friend as well. His brother Matt was another very good friend, and the oldest girl, Rita, was a carbon copy of their mother. David, who was younger, was a scamp, but perfectly decent. All her life it had only been Rafe who had sometimes made things miserable.

"I'm not your lifelong nemesis," she said softly.

His eyes seemed to darken. "You're probably right. That would be overstating it a bit. Still, we were enemies."

"Oh, yes. We *were* that."

The look they exchanged conveyed what neither was willing to vocalize—that the steamy kiss they'd exchanged earlier had redefined their tenuous relationship in ways neither could comprehend. The light changed and she turned her attention back to her driving.

"Given our past history, a little torture seems to be in order, wouldn't you say?" His tone was light, almost teasing.

She actually smiled a little. "That means I have to find a way to torture you back."

He groaned. "You're carrying this women's lib thing a bridge too far, don't you think? You've already done your own small part in ruining my weekend."

"Because I won out over your idea?"

"Yes. I consider it a downright disaster, believe it or not. We've got to win this contest and your idea won't do it."

Was he purposely trying to put her back up again?

Well, she wasn't going to take the bait. Drawing in a deep breath, she went on calmly. "Tell me why it's so important."

He stared at her as though she'd asked him why bread came in loaves. "You can ask that?"

She glanced at him sideways. "It's for your father, isn't it?"

His face darkened. "Look…"

"No, it is, isn't it? You have to come back waving a trophy for your father. Don't you?"

He slumped in his seat. "You don't know what you're talking about."

"Yes. I do. I used to be part of the family, remember?" She sighed. "Rafe, why bother to deny it? You've always had this thing about your father. And your father has always used it to play you off against Matt and…"

"That's enough, Shelley," he said, his voice tight and hard as a diamond.

But inside he wasn't so hard. She was bringing things up into the light that he would rather stayed buried. What good did it do to hash this stuff over endlessly? Things were the way they were and you had to deal with them that way. Yeah, his father could have been more understanding. He could notice how well Rafe could handle the company business once in awhile, instead of always looking to Matt to do everything. But he wasn't like that. So Rafe would go on, fighting and winning and handing his father proof he didn't really want to see. Until someday….

Oh, hell. Why had she brought this all up, anyway? He glanced at her, wanting to be angry with her, but his anger melted right away. She was so damn delicious-looking. And all she'd done was thrust some truths at him. He could handle truth. He could handle anything.

"Sorry," she said, knowing he was looking at her. "I guess I'd better learn to keep my mouth shut, huh?"

He didn't answer and she slowed, knowing they were near the address she was looking for. She fumbled for her purse and he took it from her, plucking out the paper that was sticking from the front pocket and reading out what was written there.

"It's 3457 N. Fardo, apartment 13." He grimaced. "I thought they didn't number things thirteen if they didn't have to."

"I wouldn't have thought you would be superstitious," she noted, turning on Fardo.

"I'm probably a lot of things you never thought of."

"No doubt."

He scanned the addresses. "Here we go. Left side of the street. Big orange building."

Shelley peered out in the direction he indicated and hung a U-turn to park in front of the building. Rafe looked up at it, too.

"So, I take it your friend Quinn is down on his luck?" he said softly.

She squared her shoulders and gathered her things. "Could be," she said shortly. "Now you just wait here and I'll be right back."

"Fat chance," he muttered, getting out on the other side as she got out on hers.

"Rafe…"

"You're not going into that building alone."

There was no use arguing here on the street, so she flashed him a look and let him accompany her into the lobby of the place. The walls were grubby. One of the mailboxes was hanging open. The smell of burned onions filled the air and a baby was crying somewhere close by.

"There it is at the end of the hall," she said, pointing out the door with the metal 13 on it. "You stay right here. I have to do this alone."

He nodded. He apparently knew when to stand back and give her some room.

"Stay in the hall, though," he warned her. "Don't go into the room without me."

She hesitated. That wasn't what she'd envisioned, but when you came right down to it, that was probably good advice.

"Okay," she told him, and started down the hall.

The place was creepy and she felt the hair rise on the back of her neck. She remembered Quinn as a handsome, happy-go-lucky kid with bright eyes and a ready smile. She hadn't known him well, but she would have said he was someone with a future. This place looked too dead end for that.

She knocked on the door. Nothing. After waiting a moment, she knocked again.

"Quinn?" she called.

There was no answer. Someone in another apartment opened their door a crack and looked at her, then closed it again. Taking a paper and pencil from her purse, she jotted down a quick note that included her cell number and pushed it under the door. When she turned back, she had to admit it was a relief to see Rafe still waiting for her by the entrance.

"No luck, huh?" he asked as she reached him.

She shook her head. "He's not home," she said.

They walked slowly back out into the light. Shelley noted that there was a parking area under the building. She thought about going down and seeing if she could get into it to see if a car was parked in #13's spot, but she shrugged the idea away.

"I left my number," she told Rafe as they lingered by the car, looking up and down the street. It wasn't particularly busy, but cars were going by on a regular basis, and somehow she just had a feeling… "Maybe he'll call me when he gets my note."

"Maybe."

Rafe opened her car door and she frowned at him.

"What are you doing?"

"Pretending to be a gentleman," he said with a grin.

"I suppose it's a real effort," she said, but she was smiling, too.

Standing there with the sun in his eyes, his hair so dark, his shoulders so wide, he looked like more than a gentleman. He looked like a hero. For some stupid reason her heart was suddenly pounding in her chest and she looked away from his gaze.

And that was how she noticed a blue car coming out of the underground parking and speeding away.

"Ohmigod!" she cried. "Quick, get in!"

"What?"

"Get in! Get in! That was him."

Rafe got in, barely getting the door closed before she gunned the engine and peeled out into the street.

"Hey," he said, alarmed. "What are you doing?"

"I've got to catch him," she cried, concentrating on her driving and going much too fast. "It could be my only chance."

Chapter Five

Adrenaline was pumping but Shelley felt cool and in control.

"Look, Quinn's turning up ahead," she said, squinting as she tried to cover all the bases at once.

"Shelley, take it easy," Rafe was saying, securing his seat belt and reaching around to get hers locked into place, too. "It's not like he's taking off in a plane. He'll still be there even if you don't catch him right away."

She didn't answer. Something told her she had better catch Quinn now, because he was obviously trying to avoid her and would take care she didn't find him again if she didn't do it this time.

She made the same turn the blue car had, her tires screeching on the asphalt.

"Hey, you took that corner a little fast, didn't you?" Rafe said, sounding a little unsettled.

"You just hush and hold on tight," she ordered, totally concentrated on the blue car disappearing around another corner.

"Shelley!"

"What?"

"Slow down!"

"I can't."

But she had to. Noticing pedestrians, she dropped back down to the limit, then had to stop at a crosswalk. Even catching Quinn wasn't worth risking hurting someone.

"Darn," she muttered, trying mentally to hurry the two men crossing in front of her. Her fingers drummed on the wheel. "Come on, come on."

Rafe started to say something but she wasn't listening. The way had opened up and she took it. Then she was on the highway with clear sailing ahead. The blue car had taken off and she pressed on the gas, racking up speed. She didn't look over but she could tell Rafe was staring at her in amazement. She didn't care. Her heart was racing and she was a good driver.

So there.

Quinn turned off onto a side street and she slowed to take the corner more carefully this time. They barely caught sight of him turning again a few blocks down. Shelley raced to that corner and they turned, but there was no blue car in sight.

"Which way?" she cried in anguish.

"I don't know. Turn right."

She turned right, and suddenly a huge chain-link barrier stood in her way, blocking the street.

"Whoa!" Rafe yelled.

She jammed on the brakes, throwing them both forward, but the seat belts caught them and the car careened to a stop just short of the barrier. Shelley whipped her head around, looking the other way on the street, but there was no blue car to be seen. Turning back, she slumped and they both sat still, staring at the fence and marveling that they were still alive.

Suddenly Rafe was laughing. She turned to look at him and he turned toward her. "That was one wild ride," he said, but his amusement was already fading.

His gaze dropped to her lips and she knew he was going to kiss her again. It seemed only right. Some gesture was needed, something to fit with the way her blood was pounding in her veins, the way his excitement shone in his eyes. Every nerve ending tingled as she waited, lips slightly parted, for it to happen.

He didn't hesitate. He kissed her hard on the mouth and she responded, kissing him back, her body molding into his. She knew she shouldn't be letting this happen, but it was so good. His mouth was hot and moist and delicious, and she wanted as much of him as she could get. And suddenly she wanted too much in a way she never had before. The sensation flared in her and she jerked back away from him, shocked at her own response.

"I can't believe this is happening again," she said breathlessly.

His dark eyes were searching hers. "What do you mean?" he replied, his voice husky.

"You know—kissing." She put both hands on his chest to shove him back into his seat. "You're not supposed to kiss me."

"Why not?" He was still hovering so close, she could feel his breath on her cheek.

"Because…because we hate each other, don't we?" She didn't sound as though she was sure about that.

"I don't know." He touched her chin with his finger, then leaned closer.

"What are you doing?" she asked softly, her hands completely ineffectual as they rested helplessly on his chest.

"I'm going to kiss you again."

She frowned, gathering herself together and firming her resolve. Glaring at him, she shook her head. "No, you're not. Only one kiss per car chase. That's all that's allowed."

He hesitated and to tell the truth, she wasn't sure whether she would rather he defy her or leave her alone. And when he drew back and settled in his seat again, she knew she felt more disappointment than she ought to.

So she turned her mind back to Quinn.

"Darn it all," she said. "We lost him."

"Why was he running?" Rafe asked.

She shook her head, pondering that question herself.

"I have no idea. We never had anything but a cordial relationship. In fact, we were pretty friendly at one time."

She took a deep breath and put the car back in gear, maneuvering for the return trip. Rafe watched as she turned the car around and headed back to the highway.

"Maybe there was something he didn't want to have to tell you," he suggested. "Could that be it?"

She glanced at him. "I don't see how. But I suppose anything is possible."

He grinned at her. "Whooee. That was some little adventure there, girl. I didn't know you were a drag-strip queen."

She couldn't help but smile, secretly pleased with herself.

"After all," he went on. "I was there when you learned how to drive. Remember?" He laughed. "In fact, I probably taught you a few of those moves myself."

Her smile faded. She remembered all right.

"Rafe Allman, you did not teach me anything. Your brother Matt taught me how to drive in that old Ford station wagon. With you sitting in the back seat half the time, taunting me and making me crazy."

He seemed affronted by her attitude and lack of appreciation toward his past efforts on her behalf.

"I was not taunting you. I was giving you pointers. Constructive criticism. Expert advice."

"Taunting is taunting. You were downright rude and you know it."

"Maybe you're just too sensitive. Ever think of that?"

"No. I always knew where the misery came from."
She glanced at him sideways. "And it came right from
you. You were giving me grief from the get-go. And
gosh darn it all if you aren't doing it to this day."

Rafe stared at her for a moment, then his head went
back and his laughter rang out, loud and infectious.

Shelley smiled. She hadn't achieved her goal this afternoon but she felt very good inside anyway. And she
knew darn well it had everything to do with the man sitting beside her.

"Well, look what the cat dragged in."

Shelley gave Candy an apologetic look as she entered
the small partitioned-off conference room that was
where they were to develop their campaign. She knew
the whole team must have been rudderless while she and
Rafe were out chasing Quinn through the San Antonio
streets, but they were back now and there was no time
for recriminations.

"Sorry, everybody," she said, turning to look at
what they'd accomplished so far. "We've still got two
hours before dinner. Let's use them to the best advantage we can."

"No problem, Shelley," Rafe said, giving her a wink.
"I've got things under control."

She stared at him in surprise. They'd both headed for
their respective rooms to freshen up before they re-
joined the group—or at least, she'd thought they'd both
done that. It seemed Rafe had done an end run around

her instead. Here he was with his shirtsleeves rolled up, looking like he'd been working here the whole time.

"Listen," he was saying to Candy. "I want to screen the video you took. Can you rack it up over here on this monitor?"

Shelley stepped over to his side.

"What are you doing?" she asked him, her voice low but insistent.

"Trying to get things moving here." He smiled at her, looking comfortable with the way the situation was developing. Looking like the boss.

"I'm the one who is supposed to be doing that," she told him, glancing around to make sure none of the others could hear.

But even if they couldn't hear what she was saying, they were watching, and she knew right away they were waiting to see how things were going to shake out. Either she was going to be in control, or Rafe was. Taking a deep breath, she tried to gather her strength. It was time she made a stand. But looking at Rafe, so handsome and confident, she had to wonder how she was going to do this.

"Look, Rafe, I'm supposed to be the boss. Remember?"

"Sure. I remember it well." He smiled at her. "No problem, Shelley. We'll work things out just fine."

He looked up as Dorie, the young office worker, came up to him.

"Mr. Allman," she said hesitantly, her blue eyes wide and innocent. "I did that collating you wanted done. Did you want me to go find a copy machine and make copies of the script for you?"

"Why thank you, Dorie," Rafe began, holding out his hand for the collated pages. "And yes, I do want you to go…"

"Hold it."

Shelley could hardly believe that was her voice, but as she looked around at the interested faces, she knew it had been her and that she'd said it loud enough for the entire group to hear. She was going to challenge Rafe and try—very hard—to put him in his place. Were they all going to think she was a witch when she did that? Yes, she supposed they would. But deep down, she knew it had to be done.

"I think we're forgetting what the focus of this competition is," she said, feeling a little shaky. "It's called 'Trading Places.' The whole point is for bosses and employees to switch places and bring their own unique outlooks toward solving a problem, and at the same time, begin to see things from the other side for a change. We're reversing the order of things. Getting new ideas from people in the trenches, so to speak."

She paused. The faces were all staring at her blankly. Only Rafe had a spark in his gaze. Was it anger or humor? She couldn't tell.

"We're going to be getting points on how well we do that, not how good our central project idea is," she added, mostly to Rafe. "So let's work hard on following the theme. Okay?"

Rafe looked at her, one eyebrow raised. "You think the judges aren't going to be swayed by how good the central idea is? You're nuts."

Oh, for heaven's sake! He was still hoping to get his idea used instead of hers. She couldn't believe it. She'd won the vote, but as she looked at the uncertain faces among the team, she wondered if that vote would hold if he pushed it.

"Rafe, your idea was very good, but we've decided to go with mine," she said firmly. Anger had snuffed out all shakiness now.

He shrugged and looked at her blandly. "I know that."

She gritted her teeth. He wasn't going to let this go, was he?

"If you're so crazy about your idea, why don't you give it to the B team?" she suggested. "From what I hear, they're still struggling for something to sink their teeth into."

He reacted with shock. "Give it away? Hell no. It's my idea. I'm holding on to it in case your idea falls apart."

Her jaw dropped and she had to use all her self-discipline not to let herself respond. He was being a jerk, forcing her to get tougher than she wanted to. But she knew if she didn't stand up to him now, he would make her life miserable for the rest of the weekend. And so would all the rest of them.

"Okay, here's the deal," she said, making sure everyone heard what she was saying. "For the purposes of this weekend, I'm the boss. Candy is my assistant. Rafe is Candy's assistant. I'll relay instructions through Candy. You can go to her with your problems and she'll relay them to me."

They were still waiting, standing there like cattle and she wondered if she wasn't being forceful enough. What did she have to do, scream at them all to make them understand?

"Then I guess it's back to the name thing, isn't it?" Rafe said in what she considered a slightly mocking tone. "We should all call you Miss Sinclair."

She looked at him defiantly. "Yes. For the purposes of this contest, I think that would be a good idea." She looked at the others. "If y'all are calling Rafe Mr. Allman and calling me Shelley, that sends a bad message as far as our goals are concerned. You do get that, don't you?"

A couple of them giggled, but they sobered quickly when she looked at them. Good. The aura of command was already taking hold. Either that, or they were getting ready to run for the hills. She wasn't about to let that happen. Looking around, she grabbed the script.

"Let's get going on casting for the skit, shall we? Okay, Candy, you're the mailroom girl with the heart of gold. Dorie, you're the pregnant secretary. Jerry, you're the father of the baby. Rafe, you'll play the part of the skeptical supervisor who doesn't think it's going to work."

He grinned, arms folded across his chest. "That'll be easy enough to do."

She glared at him. "Only in the end, you'll become

convinced that it's the wave of the future and you'll become one of the biggest champions of the program."

He groaned, making a face. "That'll take a little more acting ability."

"Then you'll just have to dig deep, won't you?"

He blinked and looked at her as though he was finally beginning to realize that she wasn't going to back down.

"Wow, give the woman a little power and she turns into a dictator."

He looked at her assessingly, but she couldn't help but think there was a grudging sort of respect growing in his eyes.

"Why do *you* pick and choose who gets what parts?"

She drew herself up as much as she could, though she knew it still seemed puny compared to his six-foot-two frame. Looking around, she raised her arms like a band conductor.

"Because—shall we get everyone to say it in unison?—Shelley Sinclair is the boss!"

They all muttered it with varying degrees of enthusiasm. All except Rafe.

When she looked at him with her eyebrow arched, he looked rebellious. "I won't say it."

She stared at him, hard. "You say it or you're fired."

He stared at her and she held that stare, bound and determined she wasn't going to let him win. If she "fired" him it would just be for this competition, but it would make a mark all the same. Was he going to challenge her? Was he going to force her to go through with it? Her heart was pounding. This would make or break the whole program right here.

He was staring deeply into her eyes and she knew he was trying to decide if she would hold firm. Then something changed in his dark gaze. She wondered if he was remembering the way she'd barreled down the street after Quinn's car. Maybe so, because he seemed to come to a conclusion about what she was willing to do to attain her goal, and his defiance relaxed into a smile of benign amusement.

"Okay." He threw up his hands, turning to the others, and this time he led the rest. "Let's all say it together. Shelley Sinclair is the boss."

She sighed as relief flooded over her. Something told her this was it. Rafe wasn't going to confront her any longer. At least, not about this.

"Now don't you feel better?" she said to them all.

Everyone laughed. They thought it was mainly a joke, and it was. But she wondered if they didn't pick up on the underlying thread of real antagonism between Rafe and her, because it wasn't gone, despite the adventurous afternoon they'd had together. Despite that unforgettable kiss they'd shared, the discord was very much alive. And though they'd gotten past this bump in the road, there would be others. She was going to have to be wary.

They worked on the skit for the rest of the afternoon, going over and over it, improving on it, working like a real team. Shelley was very happy with the way things were going. Rafe treated her with just the right combination of polite deference and jocular companionship. It worked. What a relief.

They adjourned to their rooms and met at the restaurant for dinner and had a rousing time. Everyone was in great spirits. The talk and the laughter ran rampant as they ate, and they lingered longer than they'd planned. Then, as they rose from dessert, Rafe came up to help her with her chair.

"So, where are we going tonight?" he murmured near her ear.

Chapter Six

Shelley turned to look at Rafe. Of course he'd guessed she would be out looking for Quinn again. There was no way to keep it from him.

"Who invited you along?" she asked, gazing at him quizzically.

"I did." He smiled at her, standing a little too close. "I'm sticking to you like glue."

She searched his eyes, wondering about him and his motivations. "Why?"

"Because you're skulking around in neighborhoods where you're going to need someone watching your back." He gave her a grin. "And I'm volunteering for duty."

They were making their way out into the hotel lobby by now. It was teeming with people returning from dinner or just getting ready to find a good late place to eat. The mood was celebratory and a bit noisy, forcing them to walk very close together in order to hear each other.

"Really?" she countered his offer of refuge. "While you're guarding me against street scum, who's going to guard me against you?"

He put a protective arm around her shoulders, helping to steer her through the crowd.

"What do you think you have to worry about me for?" he said, turning so that his mouth was very near her ear. "What do you think I'm going to do?"

She shivered. His breath touched her skin and made her want things she didn't want to want.

"I don't know," she said, feeling a little careless, a little excited. "Sell me off to the highest bidder, maybe."

He pulled her even closer. "Hey, I wouldn't ever want to get rid of you that way."

"Oh, no?" She looked up into his face. "What way *would* you want to get rid of me?"

He grinned, then pretended to think it over. "Highest bidder, huh? Got to admit, it's definitely something to think about."

"Rafe!" she wailed.

"Hey, it was a joke. You set it up so beautifully, I had to follow along." He guided her down the steps onto the walkway. "I mean, what could I do?"

"What could you do?" she echoed archly. "Say something nice, maybe. Ever think of that?"

They were outside now, the air cool compared to the

heated atmosphere inside the hotel lobby. Lights glittered up and down the street and people were scattered in groups of twos or threes. Music was coming from a dance club across the street.

He was looking down at her. "What do you consider nice?"

"Have you gone so far?" she asked teasingly, pretending great concern about his state of mind and character, "that you don't even know what 'nice' is anymore?"

He stopped and thought for a moment, actually taking her ribbing seriously, pulling her into an enclave sheltered from the general crowd by a clump of desert palms.

"'Nice,'" he said musingly, his face crumpled in concentration. "I think I remember 'nice.'" He looked down at her, a hint of humor in his dark eyes.

"Like kittens? Like the sun coming out after the rain?"

He stroked her face with his forefinger and his voice got husky.

"Like looking at a beautiful woman?"

She stared up at him and her heart did a little flip and she knew she ought to tell him to go back to his hotel room and leave her alone. She tried. She even took a very deep breath and tried very hard. But she couldn't form the words. It was just too delicious being with him this way. She couldn't resist it.

Even though she knew!

Oh, what was wrong with her? She knew this man as well as she knew anyone, didn't she? She'd known

him all her life. She'd fought with him and hated him
and tricked him and been done dirty by him. She'd seen
him being kind to his sisters and seen him being play-
ful with his brothers and seen him being loving to his
mother. But she hadn't often seen him being nice. Especially not to her.

So what was she doing here? Where was she going?
And why didn't she listen to the alarm bells that were
telling her he couldn't possibly mean it when he acted
like this?

Because she didn't want to. And that was that.

But somewhere inside she knew she was acting like
a fool. She'd been there before, hadn't she? She'd listened to Jason McLaughlin's lies and pretended to believe them. In her urgent need to find love, she'd let
herself become something she despised. How could
she risk doing something like that again? Was she really so weak?

It seemed to be the case.

"You need more, huh?" He seemed to take her silence
as a rebuff. "Okay, here goes. I'll show you nice."

He bent closer, his gaze skimming over her features
as though he were evaluating each one, and his hands
slipped up from her shoulders to cup her head lightly,
as though holding a precious treasure.

"You've somehow developed the most kissable lips
I've ever seen before in my life," he said softly.

Her heart skipped a beat but she had to pretend it
hadn't. Every muscle went limp, every instinct yearned

for him. But she couldn't let him know, now could she? So she took a deep breath and pretended to be unimpressed.

"Are you implying you think I got injections or something?" she grumbled. "Because I didn't. These are my lips, love 'em or leave 'em. They haven't changed at all since…since…"

"I'll take 'love 'em,'" he said evenly, still holding her there.

She blinked at him uncomprehendingly. "What?" she said, only the word came out like a whisper and she winced, knowing she needed an emergency implant of spine at this very moment and not sure help was on the way.

He shrugged his wide, wide shoulders. "You gave me a choice. I choose 'love 'em.'"

"Oh."

She wanted him to kiss her and she knew she couldn't let that happen. Reaching deep, she conjured up her last scrap of will and forced herself to shake off the misty sensuality that was sapping her strength. Pulling away from his touch, she tried to force a sense of exasperation where there was nothing but warm fuzziness instead.

"You're impossible to talk to," she said, gratified to hear a note of firmness in her voice she was nowhere near feeling in her heart. She turned from him. "Did you know that? You turn everything into a game. You're driving me crazy."

He gripped her arm and pulled her back to face him, leaning close. "Crazy with untamed desire?" he asked hopefully.

She sighed with relief. The aching sensuality in his eyes had been replaced by something closer to playfulness, as though he also realized they had been coming too close to the edge. If they both worked at it, maybe they could keep from falling over.

"No," she said firmly, planting two hands flat against his chest to keep him from leaning any closer. "More like unbridled annoyance. Or maybe plain old aggravation."

He stared down into her eyes as though unsure of which way he really wanted to go. She tried hard to make a stand and convince him she meant it. And to her surprise, he seemed to see that in her for the moment.

"Okay," he said, almost carelessly. And then he let her go, pulling back and shifting gears so quickly, she was dizzy.

"So why don't you let me in on the agenda," he said, looking at her expectantly, making her wonder if she'd dreamed the last few exchanges they'd had.

"O…okay." She shook her head a little, just to clear it. "It's nothing particularly exciting. I'm planning to make a visit to the Blue Basement Club."

"Sounds like a good old low-down dive."

"It's not really that bad. It's where a lot of the people I knew hung out when I first came to San Antonio after college."

He nodded thoughtfully. "You're hoping to catch Quinn there, I take it?"

She nodded. "Either that or somebody I used to know who might be able to get a message to him."

He shrugged. "Let's go."

As they walked the three short blocks to where the club she remembered was located, she bantered back and forth with him as though they were old friends instead of old enemies. As though they might be lovers. And, she had to admit, she cherished every moment of it.

They'd both changed for dinner and were dressed for the evening—Rafe in a suit cut to set off his elegantly lean body, Shelley in a little filmy dress that swirled around her knees as she walked. She knew they looked good together; she could tell by the way people looked at them.

She was falling in love with the evening, but she was hoping she could keep her head where Rafe was concerned. She was going to try very hard. After all, she had a very bad track record with men. Experience was everything in a relationship like this. Once burned, twice shy.

There was a crowd outside the club, waiting to go in. But the doorman took one look at them and let them go to the head of the line.

"Why us?" she whispered to Rafe, looking back at the envious frowns.

"Maybe he thinks we're celebrities," he said back with a laugh. His arm was around her shoulders again and he looked down. "Or maybe he thinks we're in love."

Just his saying that was electric, and not just to her. She saw it in his eyes. He couldn't believe he'd actually said such a thing. They stared at each other for a long moment, both a bit horrified, both a bit intrigued. And then the door opened and they were in the cavelike room.

The atmosphere was dark and hazy and they had to be very careful to keep from stumbling over other people as they made their way to the tiny table along the side of the room. The stage was the size of a postage stamp. A tall, lanky singer in a silky gown came out and crooned a few obscure songs in French while draping herself all over the piano, then disappeared again to a smattering of applause. The piano player filled some time with an atonal composition that seemed to be searching fruitlessly for a melody. Then a young man came out with an acoustic guitar and played some wonderful Spanish-flavored numbers.

"It's quite a mixed bag here, isn't it?" Rafe noted dryly. "From the sublime to the ridiculous and back again."

"It used to be more like a straightforward jazz club when I used to come here," she told him. "But most came to see and be seen. I'd say it's probably the same today."

"No doubt." He glanced around the room, peering into the mist at the few people he could actually see. "Any sign of anyone you know?"

"No." She did some peering as well, but nothing triggered any recognition. Returning her attention to closer at hand, she found Rafe gazing seductively at her face again.

"What are you doing?"

"Studying your features."

"What for?"

He put his hand against his chest in a pledge position and put a solemn look on his face, though his eyes were sparkling with something that could only be humor.

"I'm going to hold your image in my heart as my standard for beauty from now on. And when I meet a woman, and feel attracted, I'm going to call up the memory of your face and see if she meets the standard."

She was half embarrassed, half flattered, and she didn't know if he was doing this to throw her off guard or to "be nice."

"Rafe. If you don't stop mocking me, I'm going to get up and walk out of here."

He looked shocked that she would take it this way. "What makes you think I'm mocking you?"

"Aren't you?"

"Good Lord, no."

And the funny thing was, for a moment, she almost believed him.

"Let's dance," he said.

She frowned, holding on to her drink as though it was going to save her from something she didn't want to experience. "I don't know. It's awful crowded up there."

"That's okay." He took her free hand in his and kissed her fingers. "All the better to hold you close, my dear."

She smiled into his eyes and let him help her to her feet.

"Now you sound like the big bad wolf," she noted. "This is not reassuring."

His arms came around her and he began to sway with the music. "'Bad' has nothing to do with it. I'm a very good wolf."

No doubt about it. She closed her eyes and let the sensation of his hard warm body holding hers wash over her. She could get used to this real fast. How wonderful it would be to fall in love with a man like this and give yourself up to the emotion of it. For just a moment she let herself dream.

But then she pulled herself back with a jerk. If she was going to stay strong and resist all temptation to do some really stupid things, she was going to have to forgo the dreaming. Stick to business. Eschew all sentiment. Resist the urge to let her heart take over and plunge her into danger.

But how was she going to keep her head above water? Conversation. Think of something to talk about. For a few moments, she could only come up with things about Rafe and the way it felt to be in his arms. But gradually, her mind cleared and she remembered that this moment in time didn't exist in a vacuum. There was actually something going on back at the hotel and they were both inherently involved in it.

She looked up at him.

"I feel kind of guilty doing this while the rest of our group is slaving away making posters and editing videotape," she said, wishing her voice didn't come out quite so husky.

"You're ignoring one of the first rules of management," he told her. "Never let the underlings make you squirm."

She gave him a look. "Oh. Is that one of the axioms you live by?"

He grimaced. "Not really. But maybe you ought to adopt it for the night."

"Adopt being an overbearing arrogant boss?"

He shrugged. "Why not? It won't make you popular, but it gets results."

She would have quizzed him about his philosophy of management styles, but she caught sight of someone she recognized sitting at a table along the other side of the room and stopped short.

"Ohmigosh. There's Lindy. And I remember those two guys with her, but I don't remember their names. This is exactly what I was hoping for."

"Good." He looked toward where she was staring. "Let's go over and say hi."

They made their way across the room, threading through the tiny tables, and he didn't release her hand. For some reason, that warmed her as much as anything else he'd done that evening.

Reaching the table, she smiled at the heavyset girl with the black bobbed hair and the two young men, both sporting long ponytails and beards.

"Hey y'all. Remember me? Shelley Sinclair."

"Shelley!" Lindy leaped up and gave her a big hug.

"It's been ages!" She indicated the two men. "You remember Henry and Greg, don't you?"

"Sure." She nodded to them. "This is my friend, Rafe Allman. Mind if we join you for a minute?"

Lindy seemed happy enough to accept them, but the two men had obviously been drinking a bit too much and didn't make an effort to seem very pleased. Rafe pulled over a chair from another table for Shelley and found another one for himself. They sat and smiled. Only Lindy smiled back.

"So, you all were friends when Shelley used to live here in San Antonio," Rafe said as an ice breaker.

"Oh, yeah," Greg said, holding his glass of amber liquid high and staring at the lights coming through it. "We were great friends. We used to hang out all the time. Remember, Shelley?"

Shelley opened her mouth to agree, but he went on without waiting for her response.

"Until she hooked up with her hoity-toity friends and decided she was too good for us, that is." He put down the glass and adopted a sneer. "Suddenly she was riding around in limousines and such. Waving at us from the window like the Queen of England or something."

"Yeah," Henry agreed, looking as though the memory saddened him. "Who was that man you were living with over in that swanky high-rise?" he asked her. "Wasn't he your boss or something?"

Shelley was glad the gloom didn't allow anyone to see her redden at his words.

"Never mind that," Lindy said, kicking him under the table. "We're just glad to see you again, Shelley. How've you been?"

They chatted for a few minutes, then Shelley broached the subject of her visit.

"Do any of you still keep in touch with Quinn Hagar?" she asked.

Was it her imagination, or did a cold draft suddenly seem to be wafting about the table?

"I see him every once in awhile," Lindy admitted at last. "Why?"

"I'm looking for him. I wanted to ask him some questions about his sister, Penny. She and I were friends and roommates in college and I wanted to find out how I could get in touch with her."

The silence at the table was eerie. Looking at their faces, she was sure they were holding out on her for some reason.

"So if any of you see Quinn in the next day or so, please let him know I really want to talk to him. Okay?" She told them where she was staying, giving them the room number.

No response, although Lindy looked embarrassed and Shelley was sure she knew something. Should she play this close to the vest, or lay her cards out on the table? Considering the time element, she didn't have much choice.

"Did any of you know Penny?" she asked.

Henry frowned down into his drink and Greg stared

into space. Lindy looked at them furtively, then turned to Shelley.

"Actually, I met her a couple of times," she said. "She seemed like a nice person."

Shelley nodded. "She's great. We had a lot of fun when we were roomies."

"So…you're trying to find her again?"

"Yes. Do you have any idea where she is these days?"

Lindy licked her lips nervously but shook her head. "Not really," she said evasively.

"Too bad. Well, I heard she'd had a baby. Do you know anything about that?"

Lindy looked up, surprised. "No. I never heard that."

Shelley nodded. Lindy's candid reaction to the last question was believable but made her other answers all the more questionable. It was pretty clear that everyone here knew more than they were saying.

"I saw Rickie Mason yesterday," Shelley offered. "At Chuy's Café, where we always used to meet for breakfast on Saturdays. Remember? She found Quinn's address for me. I went over there today, but he took off when he saw me." Shelley shook her head. "We were friends once. I couldn't believe it when he ran off. Do you have any idea why he would have done that?"

She looked from one face to another, and finally they seemed to be beginning to squirm a little.

At last, Greg shrugged and glanced briefly into her face. "Maybe he thinks you're trying to get some money from him."

She made a face. "Why would he think I was trying to get money from him?"

Henry finally met her gaze. "Because everyone is always trying to get money from him. He's been in some…" He paused, obviously making a great effort on the next few words to overcome the handicap of being too tipsy to speak easily. "Fi-nan-cial diff-i-culties lately." He looked pleased that he'd come through okay. "Played a little fast and loose with the loan sharks and some big boys are after him, from what I hear," he added wisely.

"In that case," Rafe interjected mildly, "tell him there will be some money in it for him if he shows up and tells Shelley what she wants to know."

"I'd really appreciate it if you could relay that message for me," she said, throwing Rafe a grateful look.

Lindy knew something. She was avoiding Shelley's gaze and that was a sure sign of it. They lingered a few moments longer with Shelley hoping Lindy would decide to go ahead and tell what she knew. But that didn't happen and finally they excused themselves and went back to their own table. Rafe ordered another pair of drinks and they sat without speaking for a few minutes.

Finally Rafe grabbed her hand and held it tightly. "Look. So you lived with Jason McLaughlin for a while. It's no big deal."

She looked up with a smile a shade too bright. "What makes you think that's what's bothering me?" she asked him.

"Because I saw your face when that guy mentioned it. Shelley, it's really no big deal."

She drew air deep into her lungs and let it out slowly. "You're wrong. It's a very big deal." She looked at him, wondering if she could make him understand. "Because it's emblematic of all the bad choices I've made in my life."

"You're not exactly the Lone Ranger in making bad choices." His smile was gentle and completely sympathetic. "That's what growing up is all about, learning from mistakes."

She winced. "Yeah, well, mine are doozies."

He was silent for another moment, then leaned closer.

"Listen, Shelley, you didn't exactly have the ideal home and family life, as I remember. Your mother was busy trying to run that restaurant almost by herself. That didn't leave her much time to pay any attention to you and your little girl needs."

"I know," she said, feeling suddenly a little weepy. "My poor mother."

He played with her fingers. "You don't harbor secret resentments?"

She looked at him in surprise. "Toward my mother? Good grief, no. She is the hardest working woman I know. It wasn't her fault that my father abandoned us."

He nodded.

"Not only that," she went on, giving in to the impulse to unburden herself of pain from the past. "I kind of broke her heart by taking up with you people."

His smile disappeared. "What do you mean?"

She shrugged, almost wishing she hadn't mentioned it. What was the point, after all?

"She…well, she sort of felt like I'd chosen you over her. There was one time I remember when I was in high school—we were talking late at night and she just sat there and cried. She thought I'd pretty much given her up as a mother and attached myself to the Allmans, turning to your family for my nurturing. And I couldn't really deny it." Her voice shook slightly and she closed her eyes for a moment. "I know that hurt her deeply. But it was the truth."

"You *were* always underfoot in those days," he agreed. "I remember asking my father once—when I was particularly annoyed with you for some reason—if we'd adopted you yet."

She looked at him and smiled, though her eyes were brimming with unshed tears. "*You* were annoyed with *me?* I can't imagine that happening. I was such an angel."

"Really? Then I must have you confused with some other Shelley Sinclair who practically lived at my house."

"Must be."

He smiled into her eyes and she melted a little. There was something about his smile that seemed to wrap itself around her and warm her in a way no one else's smile ever had.

"Did that change things with your mother?" he asked. "Getting it out in the open, I mean."

She nodded. "In a way. I know I tried harder to let her know how much she meant to me." Her smile was rueful. "But I still got out of Chivaree as fast as I could."

He laced his fingers with hers. "How about now?"

"Now?"

"You're living with her, aren't you?"

"Yes. And I'm also helping out at the restaurant every chance I get." She sighed. "I'm trying to give her a little bit of breathing room. I'd like to make enough money so that I could get her to sell out and take life easy. I could take care of her for a change."

His fingers tightened on hers. "You're a good daughter."

"Am I? I'm not so sure of that."

They danced again and Shelley noticed Lindy and her friends were gone. Scanning the crowd, she didn't see anyone else she knew.

They left soon afterward. The crowds had thinned by the time they wandered their way back to the hotel. The air was soft and warm. A fresh breeze was coming off the desert. They didn't want to let the evening end. Lingering outside under the trees, they talked softly about inconsequential things, and then Rafe got serious for a moment.

"Okay, you want to tell me what this is about—a baby?"

She looked up, startled. "Oh. Yes. It seems Penny had a baby."

"I see." He was quiet for a moment, but when she didn't go on, he added, "So this is what you're really chasing after, isn't it?"

"Yes."

He waited a moment, and when she didn't add anything to the one word answer, he looked at her in exasperation.

"Do I have to drag every detail out of you? Come on, Shelley. You can trust me with the truth."

She sighed. There didn't seem to be much point in holding out any longer. And he was right. Though she wouldn't have been able to say that a day or so ago. But now that they'd spent some time together, she did trust him.

"Okay, I'll tell you the whole thing."

Except for one little detail, and that was something she was not at liberty to divulge. She couldn't tell him that the person she was doing all this for was his own brother.

"My friend—the one who started all this—just found out recently that his old girlfriend, Penny Hagar, had a baby shortly after they broke up. He'd never known she was pregnant. He assumes this must be his child and he wants to know what happened to it. Knowing the child exists is torturing him. He feels a huge sense of re-sponsibility and wants to do what he can for the child, especially if Penny needs any help or whatever."

He was silent for a moment, nodding slowly as he di-gested the information.

"Okay," he said at last. "Now that there's more form to this search, maybe I can help a little more directly. So…tell me who this man is."

She shook her head, wishing he wouldn't ask. "I can't do that."

He grimaced. "Okay, tell me this. When it comes out— and you know it's eventually going to come out—who you're talking about, how am I going to feel about it?"

She started to answer and then stopped herself, glaring at him.

"Oh, no, you don't. You're trying to trick me. You're trying to get me to talk about it and then you're going to start pulling facts together to try to figure out who it is, aren't you?" She turned away. "No. I'm not going to say another word about it."

"Shelley, Shelley, you're so suspicious of my motives. I'm just trying to help you."

She stared off into the night, looking stubborn.

"So what's your game plan about finding Quinn?"

She sighed. "I hope the promise of money will bring him out of the woodwork," she said. "That was a good idea you had there."

"I'm full of good ideas."

"No doubt."

He grinned down at her and she couldn't help but smile back.

Taking her by the shoulders, he gazed down into her eyes. "I really, really want to kiss you," he said.

Her breath caught in her throat but she kept her cool, flipping her hair back pertly. "You already did."

He frowned, looking a bit puzzled. "A kiss is not usually a once-in-a-lifetime thing, like climbing Mt. Everest or parachute jumping. Just because I've done it once doesn't mean my quota is filled for all time."

She looked away. "I don't think we need to revisit that territory."

His eyes narrowed. "I see." He thought for a moment, then went on philosophically. "So you're looking at it as a goal to be attained, after which one would sit back and rest on his laurels."

He slid his fingers into her hair, tilting her face up toward his, and went on in a lower voice. "Whereas I see it more as a carefully achieved milepost toward bigger and better things."

She looked up into the laughter that she knew she was going to find in his eyes, but she noticed something else there, too, something that made her pulse race a little faster and made her think of how good his body would feel against hers.

"That's the crux of the disagreement right there," she said quickly, pulling away from him, wanting to forestall any further move on his part. "And that's why we'd better consider this evening over."

Turning, she started toward the entrance to the hotel and he followed her. He caught up with her and held the door.

"Would that be so terrible?" he asked softly as she passed him.

She took a deep breath and turned to face him as they reached the elevators.

"Terrible isn't the word I would use," she said, glancing around to make sure there was no one else in earshot. "Inappropriate would fit a bit better, I think."

He frowned. "Why?"

"I'm the boss. I can't take advantage of you that way."

He threw his head back and laughed and when she met his gaze again, she could see a certain respect for her that made her heart sing.

Why was it so important that he respect her as a person even while he was attracted to her as a woman? She wasn't sure, but she knew it was one of the most important things of all. And to feel that she had that, at least a little bit, made sure that all the rest of it wouldn't be devalued in the end.

"So what does that mean?" he was asking her as they got into the elevator car. "I have to wait until Monday before I can attempt any sort of intimacy with you, no matter how innocent?"

"Hmm." She pretended to think about it, then frowned. They reached their floor and got off and she started toward her room. "No. Sorry. That won't work, either."

Reaching into her pocket, she produced her plastic room card and pushed it into the slot. "On Monday the inappropriateness turns in the other direction and it would be *you* taking advantage of *me.*"

Her door opened and she turned to smile impishly at him.

His answering grin was endearingly lopsided as he leaned with one arm against her doorway.

"You know what? This inappropriateness thing is a dodge. You're trying to avoid being kissed."

She laughed right up into his face, backing into her room and beginning to close the door.

"And tell me, kind sir," she said through the narrowing opening, "what gave you your first clue?"

Chapter Seven

Rafe tilted his chair back on two legs and watched the others going through the paces of their part of the skit. He had to admit it was getting more coherent each time they ran through it. He still thought his idea would have been much better, but he'd just about resigned himself to the fact that Shelley's idea was pretty good, too.

Now he just had to come to terms with the fact that he was enjoying everything about Shelley. Everything.

Watching her now as she directed the skit, he had to grin. She was a natural leader. It was probably a good thing that this competition had given her the chance to show how good she was at organizing and motivating people working for her. How long would it have taken for the management at Allman Industries—or even he himself—to recognize the leadership qualities she possessed if she'd never gotten this opportunity to showcase them? He was definitely going to find her a more effective position when they got back on Monday.

"Hey, kiddo," he called to her softly as she passed his way, heading for some items she planned to try out as background props. "I've got something to tell you."

She turned back, her eyes bright, but then pretended to look very stern. "If this is about that kissable lips thing again I don't want to hear it," she claimed.

He grinned. "Naw—I'm saving that sort of talk for later, when I get you alone."

"Rafe!"

"Nothing that exciting, actually. I just wanted to let you know that Matt called on my cell a few minutes ago. Pop's on a tear. He's getting all het up about this competition and he's sending Matt to help out. He'll be here tomorrow."

"Oh." She sank into the chair beside his. "Oh, Rafe, I'm sorry."

He looked at her blankly, not sure why she was suddenly brimming with sympathy.

"You don't have to be sorry. It's okay. Matt can't be on the team, but he might be able to give us some pointers. He'll have a fresh outlook."

She sat back. "Okay," she said carefully. "Then you're happy about this?"

"Why shouldn't I be? Matt can be a big help." He

studied her curiously. "I thought you and he were such good friends."

"We are," she said quickly. "It's just…well, your father is always trying to shove him into the limelight. I just thought…"

So that was it. He allowed himself a silent groan. He should have known. Shelley's theory again—that everything he did was driven by his reaction to his father's preference for his older brother.

And he had to admit, there was a sting involved. Did he ever let it interfere with his relationship with Matt? He let the question linger for a moment, but he didn't want to deal with it. Wincing, he pushed it away.

"Shelley, I'm not jealous of my big brother," he said with more bravado than conviction.

She stared at him. "Are you sure?"

He laughed a bit awkwardly. "Yeah. I took a poll. Every part of me agreed." Reaching out he took her hand. "Hey, I appreciate the concern. But it's not necessary. Matt and I are cool. We always have been. Don't worry about it."

He could see that she wanted to explore the issue further. Women! They always wanted to probe for motives and reasons why. He was going to have to train her to live a little more for the moment. Take things lightly. Go with the flow. Just as soon as he learned how to do that himself.

"What time is he coming?" she asked, obviously swallowing other things she would like to have said.

"Early in the morning, from what he said."

She made a face, thinking out loud. "Oh, darn. I haven't talked to Quinn yet."

He blinked at her, not making the connection. "What does that have to do with Matt coming?"

She looked startled, then evasive. "N…nothing. Nothing at all. I was just saying…you know, my day is pretty full."

Her face changed and she rose from her chair.

"Hey, lazy. Come on. I plan to get a lot more work out of you before lunch. I really need that tape of the school children to be edited down a little."

Going back to her original objective, to bring out more props, she set a large mirror up on an easel and stood back to see how it looked.

"The tape is full of some really cute stuff but it's too long for the segment I want to use it in. We have to stay within seven minutes for the entire program. So many things are going to have to go."

Looking up, she threw him a quick smile, then looked back at the mirror, adjusted it and checked to see how it looked from the audience level.

"That's the hard part. We're going to be cutting things ruthlessly." She narrowed her eyes, looking at the mirror placement from another angle.

"Well, hold on just a minute here, boss," he drawled, following her. "I don't think tape editing is in my job description. I haven't had the proper training for it. I'm not so sure I should be doing it."

She turned to look at him, exasperation flickering in her eyes. Putting her head to the side, she tapped his shoulder with her pencil.

"Edit tape," she said crisply, "or turn in your resignation. Either way. Your choice."

He scowled at her, his arms folded across his chest. "Killjoy," he muttered.

She grinned, then stifled it and became the boss again. "Okay, here's the tape. The editing equipment is in the audiovisual center. Let's go. Time's a-wastin'."

He lingered another moment. She'd warmed to him, hadn't she? She was feeling loose. It might be worth a try to see if she would reconsider his idea. It was such a great idea and he knew it would blow away the competition. That need to win was hanging over his head. This was probably his last chance to bring it up and hope for any sort of favorable reaction.

"You know, it's not really too late to think about using my proposal for the competition," he told her. "It wouldn't take many props and I've pretty much worked out the…"

Shelley's eyes flashed pure fire.

"Why can't you just adjust to reality and get behind this one hundred percent?" she said earnestly. "We're doing my idea. And if it's really so important to you to win this competition, you'd better get busy and make sure we do."

Turning, she grabbed a pair of scissors and began cutting up construction paper, getting ready to work on a set piece and making sure he knew she was ignoring him.

He stared at his own reflection in the glass of the large mirror on the easel.

She's right, you know, the reflection told him wisely.

He growled at the image staring at him. Of course she was right. He knew that. He took the tape, gave her one last long lascivious look that she purposefully ignored, and headed off to work on the editing. Even he could tell when the boss had just about had enough of his fooling around.

They were working very hard and Shelley was getting very nervous. When this had all begun, she hadn't cared very much about winning the competition. She certainly cared about doing a decent job, and not embarrassing herself or her company, but winning? It seemed a bit pointless.

But that was before she realized how much winning meant to Rafe. She knew it had more to do with proving something to his father than anything else, but that was important to him. And now, things that were important to him were important to her. She'd seen the way his father had ignored him time and time again when they were kids. It was always Matt he looked to in the past. It was Matt he wanted to take over the company, not Rafe, who was so much better for the job. And the irony was that Matt didn't want any part of the company.

So now she cared whether or not they won. In fact, they had to win—for Rafe, at the very least. She wanted first to prove to him that her idea would work out, and second—well, she just wanted him to be happy.

But she was worried. The few hours they had left didn't seem enough to do the work a really good job would require. Some of the set pieces she'd wanted were going to be impossible to get done in time. And the special shirts they were supposed to wear in the competition as part of the Allman team hadn't arrived yet.

Each team entry had its own style and color of shirt, advertising their company. It was all part of the theme. Without the shirts, she was afraid they wouldn't even place in the contest. Still, the gang was working really hard and she was pleased with the effort they were making.

It was a bit disturbing to find monitors from the conference committee peering over her shoulder every now and then. They were watching how well each team dealt with the boss-employee switch, which was the theme and the main competition point, so they had to be tolerated. But it made things awkward now and then.

Still, the weekend had turned out to be more fun than she'd expected. The way she'd dreaded having to work with Rafe seemed almost quaint now. They still had issues between them, but he was becoming a presence in her life in a way she had never dreamed he would.

She hadn't gotten in touch with Quinn yet, though she'd spent a long half-hour that morning calling every number she could think of that might give her a lead. Luckily she'd been able to avoid coming face-to-face with Jason McLaughlin again. In fact, most of the time she didn't even remember that he was there. That sure was a change from the old days when he'd been her major obsession.

And working on this project had given her a lift she'd never expected either. She was actually finding out she was pretty good at organizing people and getting things done, and the team seemed to turn to her naturally now, as though they sensed she knew what she was doing. If only that were completely true! There were so many loose ends to tie up at all times.

The team was working out well, though she'd found out that a few of them took off and went out clubbing with some members of team B and even some of the other teams the night before. It seemed little Dorie had been quite the party girl, if the snippets of conversation she'd overheard this morning were true. She didn't know exactly what the girl had been up to, because people tended to stop talking about it when they noticed she was near. Still, she couldn't really say much since she'd been out at a club last night as well. And everyone had shown up for work bright and early so there didn't seem to be any harm done.

All in all, things seemed to be going well. But she had enough experience to know that a crisis was likely lurking on the horizon.

Rafe hadn't returned yet with the newly edited tape when Candy answered a phone call and pumped her fist into the air, hung up and crowed, "The shirts are here! Someone has to go up to the main lobby and pick them up right away."

"Oh, thank heavens," Shelley said. Maybe it was a sign that things were going to be okay after all.

"Oh, I can hardly wait to see them!" Dorie said happily.

Shelley grinned, peeling off the plastic gloves she'd been using while gluing a sign together. "I'll go get them. I'll be right back and we can all try them on."

The conference rooms were on the lower level, so she had to take the elevator up to get to the main lobby. She was heading for the concierge desk when she heard someone call her name and she turned to see who it was.

"Jason!"

He snagged her arm before she could get her bearings and pulled her into a side alcove.

"Shelley, Shelley," he said seductively, his eyelids drooping over a gaze that was completely suggestive. "I've been looking for a chance to get you alone. We really need to have a good long talk, you and me."

Shelley glared at him. Deep inside, her system was shivering with revulsion.

"I'm busy, Jason. Our shirts were sent to the wrong hotel or something and they've finally arrived, so I'm picking them up and…"

"Come on, Shelley baby." His hand was rubbing up and down her arm. "We need to escape this rat race for a little while and talk over old times. Dredge up some old memories." He raised an eyebrow significantly. "Try out some old moves."

She stared at him. He was still an attractive man, but the sleaziness was beginning to show through the veneer of playboy good looks. Especially in the eyes. How blind had she been not to notice that before? His eyes were cold, mean, humorless. She thought of Rafe's warm gaze and Jason's absolutely repulsed her.

"Doing anything with you is the last item on my agenda, Jason. We've said all we need to say to each other and we did it long ago."

She tried to pull away from him, but his grip on her arm only tightened.

"You know there's still a spark between us. Can't you feel it tugging on you?"

This couldn't be the technique that had stunned her into blind adoration over the years—could it? She must have been crazy. And very, very dumb.

"Sparks don't do much tugging," she told him tartly, taking him literally just to annoy him, "not having the arms that would require."

"What?" He stared at her blankly, not getting it.

She sighed impatiently. "No, Jason. That's not a spark you think you see. It's a smoldering fire—a fire of resentment at what you put me through that summer."

He looked shocked at her reaction, as though no one had ever rejected his advances before. "Hey, listen honey, that wasn't really my fault. If you had just waited a few weeks, I could've gotten rid of Frances and…"

He was talking about getting rid of his wife in order to take up with his mistress again. The man was scum. And what was she for having fallen for this stuff in the old days? It made her feel like she needed a long, hot shower and a lot of lather from some gritty soap.

"Let go of me, Jason," she said evenly.

His grip was so tight it was starting to be painful. She glanced around, wondering where all the people were. She might have to start yelling if this didn't stop soon.

"This isn't amusing."

"No, Shelley," he said, his voice still smooth but his touch getting rough. "You're not being reasonable. You have to give me a chance to explain."

She tried to twist away but his sinewy strength was too much for her. "Jason, this is going to get ugly if you don't…"

Another hand reached in and took hold of Jason's wrist in a move that was obviously meant to inflict pain, and his grip on her arm came loose right away.

"Hey!" Jason cried out, jerking back.

"Touch her again and I'll break your neck."

Shelley was breathless. It had happened so fast. Rafe was there and Jason was backing away.

"You know," he was saying spitefully, rubbing his wrist, "you Allmans really should learn how to act in civilized society."

"If you McLaughlins are the product of civilized society," Rafe retorted, "I'll stick to my low-life ways. And I don't need you giving me etiquette lessons." He slid his arm around her. "And neither does Shelley."

"Oh," Jason said sarcastically. "You speak for her now?"

"Yes," Shelley said loud and clear. "He can speak for me any time he wants to."

Jason looked resentful and shrugged as though it was all the same to him. "We'll see how you feel about that tomorrow," he said. "After the competition." His grin was mean and humorless. Turning, he disappeared around the corner.

Rafe looked down at her. "What did he mean by that?"

She shook her head. "Who knows." Looking up, she smiled and without hesitation, threw her arms around his neck and hugged him tight. "I'm so glad you showed up. Thank you, thank you, thank you!"

"Anytime," he said, but the way he hugged her in return didn't seem as enthusiastic as she would have expected. "What happened, anyway?"

She pulled away. "I was coming down to get the shirts and Jason waylaid me. That's all."

His dark gaze was searching hers, studying her face, looking for answers.

"So what's the deal?" he said softly. "Do you still have feelings for this guy?"

"No, Rafe," she said earnestly. "I swear I don't. Not in the least."

He wanted to believe her but he felt a wariness he didn't even understand himself. "Then what's up with the reaction I see in you?" he asked carefully.

Reaction? For a moment she wasn't sure what he was referring to. How could her reaction look like anything but revulsion? But maybe it wasn't the current reaction he was talking about. Maybe it was what he'd noticed in her over the years.

"It's just…" She licked her lips, wanting to get this right. "It's impossible to erase all the feelings the years build up in you. Don't you think?"

He stared at her, waiting for her to explain.

"Jason was a big part of my life at one time. I can't pretend otherwise. You wouldn't believe the huge crush I had on him in high school. It was major. So when I came to San Antonio and got a job in his company, I was on cloud nine." She stopped herself, wishing she hadn't gone that far.

He waited, not sure he wanted to hear this but knowing he had to. Her words were like daggers in his soul.

He'd had old girlfriends, too. So she'd had a crush that turned into a lover. So what? Most of the women he'd ever been with had experienced much the same and it had never bothered him before. Looking back, he hardly remembered much about any of them. Not many stood out or meant anything to him now. In fact, over the years he'd begun to wonder if falling in love was just something he wasn't set up to do. It didn't happen. And now…now this. Now Shelley.

What was different about her? Why was she able to reach inside him and take hold of his heart, twist his emotions in a way no other woman ever had? He didn't know. But he listened as she finished her explanation, even though it was the last thing he felt like doing.

"So I spent some time with Jason," she said, talking quickly, wanting to get this over with. "And I wish I never had. But I did. And it didn't take long to realize that was all wrong. But it took a little longer to realize *he* was all wrong. That he wasn't worth the effort. That he's a jerk. Far from having warm feelings for him, I really can't stand the man. I hope I never have to have any dealings with him again."

He nodded, but his gaze was clouded. "Okay. Thanks for being honest with me, Shelley. I appreciate it." He gave her half a smile. "Hey, I came down to help you with the shirts. Let's go get them."

She took his arm and they started toward the concierge desk. But something fluttered uneasily down inside her. Something about the way Rafe had taken her explanation hadn't quite jelled. He wasn't completely convinced. What could she do to prove it to him?

The shirts were a big hit. Soft blue and made of a great grade of cotton, they had the Allman logo over the pocket and a picture of a winery on the back. Surprisingly everyone had the right fit. They paraded in front of a long mirror and admired themselves. They looked like a real team.

Shelley looked at her watch. "Oh, gosh. Now we have to take out an hour for lunch. We can't afford to do that!"

"Don't worry," Rafe told her. "I made an executive decision and ordered in pizza. We won't have to leave the room."

"Oh, you're a lifesaver. That is the perfect solution. We'll have pizza but keep right on working." She smiled at him. "I knew it would pay off having you around."

"I exist but to serve."

She was happy to see the humor back in his eyes.

"Okay, everybody," she called out when the pizza arrived. "Have some lunch but we can't slack off. The schedule for dress rehearsals has been posted and we've got the 6:00 p.m. slot. We've got to be ready by then."

There were groans all around.

"We'll work right up to five and then I want all of you to go to your rooms and get a nice hour's rest. Okay?"

"Hey," Rafe said about an hour later, motioning with a nod of his head, "It looks like you've got a visitor."

Looking up from the background poster she was painting, she saw Lindy smiling from the hallway.

"Hi!" she called, waving a paintbrush. "Just a second."

Rafe took the paintbrush from her and she wiped her hands on a towel, then went out to join her old friend in the hall.

"I'm so glad to see you."

Lindy looked around a little nervously. "I wanted to talk to you for a minute. Can we take a walk around the courtyard?"

"Sure."

Shelley glanced back at Rafe. He nodded, knowing she was silently asking him to take over and keep things moving. Amazing how they had gone from animosity to silent communications in a matter of days.

She and Lindy went out into the courtyard. Landscaped to remind guests of a tropical island, it was filled with lush greenery and palms, with an aviary full of chattering birds along one side and a sculptured swimming pool down the middle of the area. Small waterfalls fed into the pool and the sounds of the tropics came from loudspeakers hidden in the bushes. Shelley took Lindy's arm and they began to make their way through the jungle.

"I had to come and see you," Lindy began, pushing her shiny dark bangs aside and smiling at Shelley. "I'm sorry I was so remote last night, but I couldn't really talk in front of Henry and Greg," she said apologetically. "They and all of that group have this whole us-against-them mentality. You must remember how they are."

"Oh, yes." Shelley stopped just short of rolling her eyes.

"They consider you a traitor of sorts, you know. Because you dumped us and went off with your boss like you did. They think you sold out."

"I know that's how they feel. And I don't blame them for being annoyed about that. I'm annoyed at myself for doing it." She looked at the dark-haired woman, wondering about her and about her life. "How about you? Do you feel that way, too?"

"Of course not. I always liked you, Shelley."

Shelley smiled at her. "So when are you going to move on, Lindy?" she said.

Lindy shrugged. "I've had my ups and downs. I won't be hanging around here forever."

"I hope not." She squeezed her arm affectionately. "You've got a lot of potential. But I'm sure you hear that all the time and I don't want to lecture you. So, what did you come over here to tell me? Have you talked to Quinn?"

"No." She shook her head. "I tried but he's not answering his phone. I think it's disconnected. But I can tell you something about Penny."

She licked her lips, giving Shelley a worried look, then looked around and spotted a bench. "You'd better sit down. This isn't going to be easy."

"What?" Shelley didn't sit down, but she grabbed Lindy's arm again, a quiver of alarm racing through her system. "What is it?"

Lindy took a deep breath. "Penny died over a year ago."

"What?" Shelley gasped and did slide down onto the bench after all. "Oh, no. What happened?"

Lindy dropped down to sit beside her.

"Pancreatic cancer. It came on very suddenly and she was gone in a couple of weeks."

"Oh, that's terrible." Shelley put her hands over her face and rocked back and forth. "Poor Penny. Poor Quinn." Dropping her hands, she looked at Lindy. "And the baby?"

Lindy shook her head. "Honestly, Shelley, I never heard of any baby. If Penny had a baby, she didn't talk about it. And Quinn never said a word."

Shelley stared at her. "Then where could the baby be?"

Lindy shrugged. "Are you sure there really was a baby?"

Slowly shaking her head, Shelley sighed. "I'm not sure about anything, to tell you the truth."

"I take it you know the father."

"Maybe. If there *is* a baby."

They were both silent for a moment, awed by the forces of life that seemed so overpowering and unpredictable. Lindy looked at Shelley.

"You still need Quinn to find out more, I guess."

Shelley winced. "And Quinn doesn't want to be found."

"No." Lindy gave her a quick, mischievous smile. "But you seem to have found a new man to make your life more interesting. I've gotta say, I approve. I was so jealous last night. You both look like you're so in love."

"In love?" Shelley's world rocked for just a moment. "Rafe and I?"

Lindy shrugged. "That's the way it looked. I watched you when you were dancing." Her mouth turned down at the corners. "So it's not a romance? Too bad. He's a hottie."

A romance—with Rafe? The thought boggled the mind, and yet it sent out tentacles of interesting emotions at the same time. A romance with Rafe. Why not?

Oh, for Pete's sake—there were a thousand reasons!

Chapter Eight

*H*e's *a hottie.*

The words kept running through Shelley's mind and she couldn't shake them. Every time Rafe was near, she didn't have to look up to see him, she could feel his presence. And in her mind the words came again. *He's a hottie.*

That was fine for hotties, of course, but tough luck for dumb fools who fell for them.

It was almost an hour later, long after Lindy had gone, that she managed to get Rafe off to the side and tell him what she'd learned. He was almost as stunned as she was, which warmed her. After all, he didn't even know Penny. They mulled it over for a short time, talking softly, knowing they had to get back to work but lingering together for a few moments more. He reached up and brushed her cheek with the palm of his hand, his dark eyes filled with sympathy.

Oh, he's much more than a hottie, she thought to herself.

And then he noticed something at the other end of the hall and his eyebrows went up. "Look. Matt's here. I guess he decided to come on down instead of waiting for morning."

"What?" Shelley whirled and searched the hall, spotting him right away. "Oh, no!" Turning back, she grabbed Rafe's lapels in anguish. "Oh, Rafe, how am I going to tell him?"

He frowned down at her. "Tell him what?"

She pulled back, her face mirroring her realization of the mistake she'd made, and his own face cleared with sudden comprehension.

"Oh, man. Do you mean to tell me Matt is this friend you've been talking about? Matt and Penny…?"

She shook her head, eyes closed, sick at heart. It was all too much. "You're not supposed to know this," she mumbled miserably.

But it was too late. And Matt was approaching fast.

"Hey there, bro, good to see you," Rafe said. Matt gave him a hug and smiled down at Shelley.

"Do I get a hug from my favorite girl?" he asked.

She felt close to tears but she hid it and threw her arms around his neck, hugging tightly. "Oh, Matt!" she wailed.

"Hey, what is it?" He pulled back and looked at her stricken face. "Did your team get disqualified from the competition or something?"

She shook her head. "Much worse than that," she said, taking his hand and looking up into his dark eyes, so like his brother's. "I've got some terrible news."

Rafe gestured to them both to follow him and he led the way out into the courtyard. Luckily it was empty and they could talk privately.

Quickly and precisely, Shelley gave Matt the details, watching as he turned an ashen color. She explained how she knew about Penny's death and related the fruitless search for Quinn.

When she was finished, Matt merely said, "The baby?"

She explained that they didn't know much and what they had heard was merely speculative. "We really need to find Quinn so we can get the whole story," she said.

She exchanged a glance with Rafe. Matt didn't seem perturbed at all that his brother had been let in on this secret without his permission. That was a relief. The two brothers really seemed to be closer than some people realized. There were dozens of reasons why the two of them might resent each other—especially on Rafe's side. And yet, she never saw any evidence of it. She hoped it was true and that Rafe wasn't just hiding it well.

Matt was obviously shaken. Rafe gave him a half hug and he tried to smile, but he couldn't quite manage it yet. Nodding slowly, he thought over all the implications of what he'd just heard.

"Take me to that apartment."

She glanced at Rafe again. They were in the middle of preparing for the dress rehearsal. How could they possibly leave the others to fend for themselves? "Right now?"

"Yes." Matt had a way of making his judgments seem eminently strong and sure. "If the three of us go, maybe we can catch him."

Rafe shrugged and said, "What do you think, boss?"

Boss. She heard the word with a start. She'd forgotten she was the boss and had to make the decision. And she could hardly believe that Rafe was voluntarily deferring to her. Bosses got to make the hard calls, but they had to take the responsibility if things went wrong, too. Did she dare chance this? She looked at her watch and took a deep breath.

"Okay. I'll tell Candy. But we have to be back by four at the latest."

Matt's car was still parked in front of the lobby and they piled in. He drove quickly but with quiet skill, following Shelley's directions without saying anything himself. Shelley's heart was fluttering in her chest. She wasn't sure what he was planning. Things were changing too fast for her.

He pulled the car over to park half a block from Quinn's apartment building. They all got out and started toward the entrance.

"I'll go down into the parking garage and find his car," Rafe said. "So he can't get out that way this time."

Matt nodded. "Got your cell on?" he asked his brother. "I'll call you when I know what's happening."

Nodding, Rafe headed for the parking garage. Shelley followed Matt into the building, pointing out Quinn's apartment. They approached it gingerly and Matt stood back away from the viewing lens's range while Shelley knocked on the door.

"Quinn?" she called when he didn't answer right away. "It's Shelley Sinclair. Please let me talk to you for a minute."

No answer.

Matt moved closer along the wall and pressed his ear to the door. Jerking upright, he pulled out his cell phone. "He's going out the window," he told Shelley. "Rafe, he's coming your way," he barked into the phone. "We'll be right behind him."

Adrenaline raced through her as they hurried back outside, running to the back of the building. As they came around the corner, they found Rafe struggling with Quinn at the entrance to the garage. Matt joined in and they had the younger man pinned to the wall in no time. Rafe got control of his arm and pulled him out to face the others.

Matt stared at him and he stared back defiantly.

"Well, Quinn," Matt said. "It's been a long time."

Quinn didn't respond. A tall, thin man in his mid-twenties, Quinn looked undernourished and overly hostile. A mop of dark blond hair that hadn't been cut for much too long crowned his head. He wore a white

T-shirt, dirty jeans and even dirtier sneakers. The total effect was less than pleasant.

"Hey, that's not very polite," Matt told him. "You should answer when you're spoken to. Need a lesson in etiquette, do you?"

Rafe jerked the arm he held behind Quinn's back and Quinn yelped in pain.

"Hey," he said. "Cut it out. There's no need for any rough stuff."

"Of course not," Matt said smoothly. "Because you're going to tell me what I want to know, aren't you?"

Quinn's head went back and his eyes narrowed, but he started muttering. "Everything's cool. I remember you, Matt. I'll talk to you."

Matt looked at Rafe. They gave each other an imperceptible nod, the sort of wordless communication brothers have with each other.

"Okay," Matt said, standing with his legs wide apart. "Why don't you start with why you keep running away from Shelley?"

The kid glanced at her and gave her a brusque nod. "Sorry, Shelley," he said gruffly. "You gotta be careful around here."

He looked back at Matt, beginning to lose the resentful pose and becoming a real person again.

"Look. I've been running for a while now. I've changed apartments three times in the last month. I don't know how you even found me."

"What are you hiding from?"

He shrugged. "Loan sharks. I got in too deep and I'd like to get out without having my legs broken."

Matt nodded slowly, studying Quinn hard. "Sounds like a worthy goal. How much do you owe them?"

Quinn hesitated, then said a figure that made Shelley's eyes widen.

Matt hesitated, then took out a pen. "Give me their names."

Quinn looked confused. "What for?"

Matt's gaze was calm and sure. "I'll take care of it."

Quinn's jaw dropped. "You'll take care of it?" he repeated incredulously.

"Yeah. It's the least I can do for Penny's brother." He gestured to Rafe to let Quinn loose, then stood poised, pen ready. "But you've got to do something in exchange."

Quinn rubbed his arm and gave Rafe a look, but he didn't seem damaged. "What is it?"

Matt glanced around at the shoddy surroundings. "Get out of this place, away from the people that keep you mired in this lifestyle. Move out of here and come to Chivaree. I'll get you a job. Maybe even at Allman Industries."

"Chivaree?" The kid was aghast. "The place is a dump. It's nowhere."

"Sure. That's what you need, a nowhere town. The kind of place where people look out for each other and put you straight when they can see you're taking a wrong road. It's somewhere you can heal and get better and become a worthwhile human being again." His gaze hardened. "You going to do it or not?"

Quinn moved restlessly, rubbing the back of his neck with one hand. "You'll pay off the loan sharks?" He looked at Matt as though he couldn't really believe it.

"I will."

There was something about the way the man said it that left no room for doubt.

Quinn moved restlessly, looking at Rafe, then at Shelley. Finally he looked back at Matt. "Okay," he said, somewhat reluctantly. "I guess I could give it a try."

Shelley watched, her heart aching. It was funny, but watching Matt be brave and compassionate and magnanimous made her like Rafe all the more. She already knew Matt was all those things. Now she was pretty sure Rafe was, too. In fact, at the moment, she was pretty crazy about the whole darn Allman family…all except for the father. Him, she could do without.

"We just heard about Penny's death today," Matt was saying to Quinn. "I'm really sorry. She didn't deserve that."

Quinn nodded, suddenly unable or unwilling to make a statement and ducking his head.

"Now," Matt said, "tell me what happened to her baby."

Quinn's head rose sharply. "Baby?" he said, looking from one to the other of them with a shifty glance.

"She did have a baby, didn't she?"

He relaxed as though he'd realized it was too late to lie about that. "Okay. You're right. Penny had a baby."

"When?"

He thought for a moment, then named a date that had Matt nodding.

"That would be about six months after we broke up," he said solemnly.

"Yeah." Quinn looked up at him and almost smiled. "She told me you were the father."

The emotion that flashed across Matt's face was indefinable, but deep and obviously painful. "Where's the baby now?" he asked, his voice rough.

Quinn shook his head and looked apologetic. "I don't have the slightest idea." He shrugged. "She gave it to someone else."

Matt looked thunderstruck. "She put it up for adoption?"

"I guess."

"What was the name of the agency?"

Quinn hesitated, scrunching up his face. "I don't know if she did anything official. She was pretty much running below the radar, if you know what I mean."

Matt was having a hard time keeping his temper now. "No, I don't know what you mean. Where the hell did she take that baby?"

"Listen, I don't know." Quinn took a step back to get out of Matt's immediate reach. "She had the kid and then she didn't have it. I never even saw it."

"There was nothing in her papers when she died?"

"Nothing I saw. I threw away most of that stuff." He looked at each of the three of them in turn. "You can look through what I kept if you want. She didn't really have much." He cleared his throat. "She didn't ever get much of a life, poor girl."

They were all silent for a long moment, paying a tribute of sorts to the woman who died too young.

But Matt had one more question. "Was the baby a boy or a girl?" he asked softly.

Quinn shook his head, his eyes luminous in the afternoon sunlight. "Sorry, Matt. I really don't know."

Shelley coughed. She had to. She'd been agonizing for the last few minutes. It was getting late and there was a competition that had to be won.

"I hate to do this," she said at last, "but we've got to get back for the dress rehearsal."

Matt turned and looked at her as though he'd forgotten she was there. "Go ahead," he said, pulling out his car keys and tossing them to Rafe. "You two go on. I've still got to get those names. Quinn can take me back to the hotel. Right?"

Quinn shrugged. "Sure."

Rafe frowned, looking as though he didn't want to leave his brother behind in this neighborhood. But if Matt was going to stay, they really had no choice. He pulled his brother aside for a moment of private conversation, then joined Shelley. They started for the street. When she looked up at his face, she found him grinning.

"What's so funny?" she asked him.

"Life," he said. "Damn." He stretched. "Matt shows

up and things start popping." He shook his head in admiration. "It's always been like that. What a guy."

She stared at him, bewildered. There truly didn't seem to be any envy in him and she found that hard to understand. It was true that Matt always came across as the winner, the best guy, the natural leader. But she'd come to realize that Rafe wasn't much different.

Still, he seldom got that kind of recognition. Especially from their father. So why didn't he resent it more?

"He's always been your hero, hasn't he?" she said softly.

He nodded. "Sure."

That was only natural on one level. Most boys idolized their big brothers. But Rafe was a man now and life had given him so many reasons to go against that trend.

"And I'll bet David looks up to you the same way," she offered.

He looked surprised. "I doubt it."

"Why?"

His mouth quirked at the corner, a sure sign he was getting annoyed with the topic.

"You deserve it," she added staunchly.

He groaned. "You've got a rosy view of life, don't you, Shelley? Haven't you figured out yet that you don't usually get what you deserve? That most things are going to flake out on you?" He shook his head, looking out at traffic. "You've only got yourself, you know. Don't go counting on anything or anyone else. There's no guarantee they'll be there for you when it counts."

She sat very still and didn't answer. There it was, the little kernel of truth that she realized she'd been searching and probing for. There *was* a resentment buried deep inside him. Much as he tried to pretend otherwise, he was only human, after all.

The dress rehearsal was a disaster. Lines that had flowed from the tongue a few hours before were completely lost. Background set pieces fell over. The VCR wouldn't work, and when it finally did, the tracking was all off. Candy walked up to the microphone for her speech, tripped and fell to the ground, sliding under the chairs and knocking them over. In flailing around to catch herself, she grabbed the corner of the tablecloth, pulling down the entire display. Dorie leaped forward to save the display and fell flat on her face as well.

"They're going down like bowling pins," Rafe said, shaking his head in resignation. "Maybe we should call for a paramedic van to be placed on call tomorrow, just in case."

Shelley closed her eyes. "A bad rehearsal means a great performance. Doesn't it?"

"And the Easter bunny lays chocolate eggs," Rafe said skeptically. "Yeah. Well, we'll see, won't we?"

Everyone was pretty gloomy at dinner. Matt didn't join them. He didn't feel much like eating and Shelley couldn't really blame him. She didn't feel much like it, either, but she felt, as the "boss," she had to be with her team. What little conversation there was seemed strained and no one ate very much.

Dinner over, the team repaired to the conference room to work on all the snags they'd come across during the dress rehearsal. It was almost ten o'clock when they finally gave up and headed for their respective rooms. Shelley rode up in the elevator with Rafe. She looked at him bleakly.

"So what do you think?" she said. "Is there any hope?"

Gazing at her steadily, he didn't answer. She closed her eyes and began to laugh. "I am so tired. I feel like the last two days have lasted about seven years."

"I know what you mean."

"This being the boss stuff isn't all it's cracked up to be, is it?"

"It has its pluses and minuses. All in all, I'd rather be in charge than being told what to do."

She opened her eyes and looked at him, not sure if she felt the same. They reached their floor and got off the elevator. He walked her slowly toward her room.

"I know you still think we should have used your idea," she told him. "And who knows? Maybe you're right. If this doesn't pan out tomorrow, I'll owe you a big apology."

He frowned at her. "Don't be ridiculous. I'm as committed to your idea as anyone now. We're going to make it work. It's got a great theme. As long as we can keep Candy from destroying the scenery, we've got a chance."

She laughed. They'd reached her door. Turning, she prepared to say good-night. "I'll meet you early," she told him. "I'm going in now and going to bed."

His eyes seemed black as coal. "Can I come with you?" he asked simply.

He'd surprised her. "Rafe…"

"Look." He touched her chin with his forefinger. "I just want to be with you for a while. No strings attached. I just want to talk and sort of get some things straight in my head. Do you mind?"

Looking up into those dark eyes she knew she couldn't deny him anything. But it might be wise to try.

"We're old friends, remember?" he said.

"Old enemies," she reminded him.

He shrugged. "Old friend, old enemies. They pretty much blend together after a while."

"You think?" She surrendered to the inevitable and opened the door wide.

He came inside her room and she felt her heartbeat quicken. He was so impossibly handsome and so completely male. A very dangerous combination. She could probably fall in love with him if she let herself. But she knew better. Didn't she?

"Would you like a drink from the little refrigerator?" she asked, pointing to the guest bar in the corner. "Or would you like a cup of mint tea?"

"Mint tea?"

"I brought my own setup. I just plug in my little jug and in a couple of minutes, boiling water for tea."

"That would be great."

She chattered on about nothing while she brewed the tea and poured it out into two mugs. Then she looked around her room and realized there weren't many places to sit that didn't bring on thoughts of intimacy.

"Let's go out on the balcony," she suggested.

"Why not?" he replied obligingly.

She turned to look into his face as they made their way out into the night air. He looked calm, pleasant and everything he was saying was so agreeable. Was this really the same Rafe Allman she'd known all her life? Even two days before, he'd countered everything she said with some sort of smart-aleck remark. Now he was like a great big kitty cat, ready to please and purr.

It was a little cool on the balcony, but she had on a long-sleeved cotton sweater and he wore a loose shirt of heavy jersey. They sat on wooden chairs with a small table between them and listened to the sounds from the street below. A mariachi band was playing somewhere, the sound of the horns sailing up through the palm trees. A piece of the river was visible if you knew where to look, and the lights of San Antonio twinkled all around. Hard as they'd worked, this had been a good weekend, an oasis from real life that was going to end in another twenty hours or so.

"So what happens when we go back to Chivaree on Monday?" she asked him softly.

"What happens? Life goes on." He shrugged, sipping

his tea. "If we win, we'll go back in triumph. And Pop will be happy."

"And if we lose?"

He was quiet for a moment, then said calmly, "We won't be triumphant. We'll tell everyone to wait until next year, just like the baseball teams do."

She was glad to hear he wasn't considering slitting his wrists over it. But that didn't really take the pressure off.

She moaned. "I'll probably get fired."

He looked at her in surprise. "Why would you be fired?"

"Because I'm the boss. If we don't win, it's my fault. Isn't that the way it works?"

He chuckled. "Don't worry. I'm not going to let anybody fire you."

She pulled her legs into the chair under her, getting comfortable. "It might not be up to you."

He grinned. "Let me tell you a little secret, lady. Most of what goes on at Allman Industries is up to me."

She knew that, but she wasn't going to admit it to him. "Maybe so. But your father is still the president of the company."

He turned and looked at her. "And you think he's still trying to get Matt to take over for him," he said dryly. "This is quite a little hobby horse you've taken on for yourself."

She twitched nervously. That wasn't what she'd been thinking, but now that he mentioned it, that was pretty much common knowledge around Chivaree. Everyone knew Jesse Allman wanted his oldest son to take over the company. And everyone knew that Matt had avoided the issue by going off to medical school and staying away for years. Meanwhile, Rafe was always there, doing what had to be done.

"Isn't he still pressuring Matt?" she asked simply.

Rafe growled at her. "Matt has never wanted to take over the business. And I've always wanted to."

"And your father has always made it very clear he thinks Matt should be the one."

He hesitated before he answered her. "Yeah. I guess it's not a secret."

She sneaked a peek at his face. "You can't tell me that doesn't bother you."

He waited a long moment before answering.

"I don't think *bothers* is the right word." He ran a hand through his thick hair, standing parts of it on end. "Sure, I wish my father would be more realistic. But it would also be nice if he didn't swear so much and stopped drinking whiskey. He's not going to change. And we all have learned over the years to work around his idiosyncrasies."

She looked over at him. His eyes looked huge and dark in the shadows. She felt an overwhelming empathy for him. It came over her in a wave and she went on with the subject, even though she knew he wanted her to drop it. Somehow she just couldn't right now. These were wounds and feelings she'd witnessed since childhood and once she'd begun to release them, it was hard to shut off the flow.

"Don't you also wish he gave you a little more credit for the great job you do running the company, instead of always trying to get Matt interested?"

"Shelley…"

"Because I do," she said, her inner anger finally showing through. "It makes me crazy to see him over-looking all that you do. I want to shake the man."

His white teeth flashed. "Don't do that. He's falling apart as it is."

She winced. The man deserved sympathy for his struggle with cancer, but that didn't give him carte blanche to treat his family cruelly. "Rafe, don't you see that you crave your father's approval as a way to make up for all this other stuff? Don't you see how it's affected your life ever since you were a child?"

"Oh, please," he said dismissively. "I'd like his approval, sure. But it's not keeping me up at night."

"Isn't it?" She just didn't believe that. "Then why this drive to win the competition? Doesn't it have at least something to do with your need to prove something to him?"

He stopped and thought, then looked up at her candidly. "Sure. There's probably some of that in there."

She nodded.

"But so what? It's all part of life. I can deal with it."

"But it bothers you."

"Okay, okay—yes, it bothers me."

He was getting annoyed with her and she didn't blame him.

"Okay, I admitted it," he said. "Are you happy now?"

She sighed. "Yes," she said, though she wasn't sure it was true.

It still didn't change anything and she wasn't sure what she'd thought she was accomplishing here. But somehow, something had to be done. Rafe deserved it.

She didn't dare bring up the other element she was sure was a part of the way he protected his heart and his feelings from too much close contact with anyone else. The pain he'd gone through over the death of his mother had to be behind a lot of the cool exterior he presented to the world. His mother had been his main cheerleader and once she was gone, he had to struggle with his father unprotected. That hadn't made it easy on him, growing up in the competitive Allman family.

"It's much better to get these things out in the open," she offered tentatively.

He groaned. "Spare me the psychology, Ms. Freud."

He stretched his legs out, looking comfortable even though she was pushing a theme he didn't want to deal with. She felt a rush of affection for him. Why had she always considered him so ill-tempered? She knew better now.

He was looking out at the lights of the city. "I suppose you're going to tie all this in with the fact that I haven't found a woman to marry," he mused softly.

"Well…" Actually, that was a bit of a touchy subject for her to be getting into.

"And you're going to tell me I can't connect with

women because my father doesn't respect my work enough."

"Well…"

"And I'm going to tell you that it's all horse manure. Because, you know what? I haven't found a woman to marry because I've been too busy running a business. End of story." He turned on her challengingly. "So what's your excuse?"

She blinked. "Pardon me?"

"Why aren't *you* married? Why can't *you* find someone to connect to?"

"I…well, I…"

"See? Not so easy when you're the one being attacked."

He was right. And she deserved what he was saying. But she didn't buy that the two of them were in the same boat. After all, she'd had a few relationships in her time. The story on Rafe was that he just didn't do that. He'd dated enough. Girls fell for him like leaves in a breeze, but as far as she knew, he'd never had one woman, one girl, to call his own. And that had to be entirely through his own choice.

"Have you ever been in love?" she asked him.

He seemed to find that a hard one. Looking out into the night, he swallowed a couple of times before he answered. "You got me there. I never have been." Turning, he fixed her with his dark stare. "How about you?"

"Me? Yes, actually. At least I thought I was in love."

"Oh. Of course. Jason McLaughlin."

He was still staring at her, and suddenly it felt as

though his gaze was boring holes in her soul. But she knew it was her own fault. After all, she was the one who had insisted on going down this road to instant personality analysis. Live by the sword, die by the sword.

"So what was that like?" he asked, his tone just this side of sarcasm. "A good experience? Did you grow as a person? Did love turn you into a more compassionate human being? Or did it turn you against romance altogether?"

She took a deep breath. She really didn't want to talk about this right now. So maybe she should have laid off him a little, too. Was that his point? Because she had to admit, he was probably right.

"You win," she said, looking up at him. "I'm sorry I pried so much. And you know what? I would really appreciate it if we didn't talk about Jason."

He grimaced, looking away. "You see, it's the way you react whenever McLaughlin comes up that makes me wonder…"

"Don't," she said shortly, stifling the fluttering in her heart. Didn't he know that it was guilt that haunted her, not affection? "There's nothing to wonder about. I can't stand the man. Now can we drop this?"

He looked at her for a long moment, then looked away.

"I guess I'd better get going. Tomorrow is the big day."

"Already?" Despite everything, she felt a sense of disappointment she hadn't been expecting.

He nodded, pushing himself to his feet and looking out at the velvet night. She rose and stood beside him.

"Whatever happens tomorrow," she said softly, "I'm really glad…"

He looked down at her and smiled, touching her cheek with the palm of his warm hand. "What? What are you glad about?"

She hesitated, wanting to keep his hand there as long as possible. "I'm glad we got to know each other better," she said softly. "I mean, I never realized…"

She looked up at him, at his dark eyes, his hard mouth, his rumpled dark hair, and she wanted his kiss more than she'd ever wanted anything in her life.

He saw the longing in her eyes but he hesitated. Kissing Shelley like this wasn't going to be a casual thing. If he took this step…if he took her trust and her heart in his hands he knew instinctively that it would mean something. Exactly what, he didn't know. But it would be a commitment of sorts.

Commitment was something he'd avoided for almost thirty years. Why would he want to give in to it now? No, it wasn't worth it. Shelley was very appealing, but she was like a human trap, lying in wait for him to take one step too far and then the string would snap and the rope would yank and he'd be hung out to dry, twisting slowly in the wind. He was too wary and aware. He wasn't going to let that happen to him.

"Better get some sleep," he said gruffly, turning away and starting into the room. "I'll see you in the morning."

She didn't answer. She was following him and just before he reached the door, he felt her touch his arm.

"Rafe?" she said softly.

He turned back, though he knew before he started to move that it was a mistake.

"Rafe?" she said again, her gaze misty, like smoke from a smoldering fire.

It was something in the sound of her voice that got him. For one second, then two, he was afraid. It shivered through him, a brief regret, a sigh, a sense of saying farewell to a part of him that was leaving now. Because once he looked back down into her eyes he was lost and he knew it. But he did it anyway. And the fear evaporated like summer rain on concrete and he abandoned himself to the inevitable.

It was bound to happen. It had been in the cards from the moment their gazes had met that first day of the conference. He had to experience her, to touch her, hold her, kiss her. And once he did that, he would know the trap was sprung.

"Shelley," he murmured, one last lingering hope of saving himself that disappeared before it was even fully formed as she reached up to touch his face with her hand.

It was such a relief to give in. She curled into his embrace as though she'd been born to please him, surrendering her warm, sweet mouth to his exploration. He took her, held her, drank from her as though he were dying of thirst. She felt so good. Every rounded part of her fit so well against every angular part of him and he pulled her closer, wanting to feel her everywhere. Each sigh, each moan, aroused him more, until he was throbbing, aching with need for her, blind and deaf to anything else but that pure building desire.

His hands slipped under her shirt, sliding up her smooth back. She felt like fine silk and tasted like an exotic wine. When he cupped her breast, feeling the nipple harden in his hand, she cried out and her whole body shuddered, as though some new force was invading it. Her responsiveness was the most provocative thing he'd ever had under his control and the sensation nearly drove him mad.

The bed was right there and they both knew it. It was a destination, a place where their need for each other could be played out in full. He was fully aware of it the whole time, and Shelley was only vaguely aware.

Still, Shelley knew what she was doing, tempting fate, tempting danger. But she'd decided she didn't care anymore. She was all feeling and she didn't want thought to intrude. She pressed her body to his and joy sang in her veins as she felt his response.

You've been here before, something inside was warning. *Don't you remember Jason? Don't you remember the agony when you realized he didn't really love you? Don't you remember the shame when you saw his wife?*

She did remember, but the memory of those things was being blotted out by the heat Rafe conjured up in her, the feel of his hands on her skin, the feel of his hard body against hers, the smell and the taste of him.

I'm in love with Rafe Allman.

What?

Yes. In love with Rafe. Forever and for all time.

The shock of that discovery jolted her and she pulled away, wiping her mouth with the back of her hand and looking at him with a sort of horror.

"What?" he asked her between labored breaths, still reaching to bring her back into his embrace. He was clearly oblivious to anything but the urgent need for her.

She stared at him in wonder. Another moment and they would have gone over the edge and into a whole new level of relationship. She wasn't ready for that. She couldn't risk it. Not yet.

"I think you'd better go now," she said, backing away.

Catching himself, he took a deep breath. His blood slowed and his brain reengaged.

"Shelley, I'm sorry," he said quickly. "I promised you this wouldn't happen."

She shook her head. "No, no, it's my fault. But I just didn't realize…"

"What?"

"How important it would be," she said softly, willing him to understand.

He frowned, puzzled, but slowly his face cleared. He got it. He'd been thinking something very close to what she was saying, hadn't he? That was when he realized she was as scared of this as he was.

Looking at her, he gave her his most crooked smile. "Shelley," he said, touching her hair with his hand, letting his affection for her show in his dark eyes. "Shelley, you're very special to me."

She nodded. "You, too," she whispered. Taking his hand, she pressed a kiss into the palm, closing her eyes.

"I'd better go," he said, reluctant but determined to do the right thing for once. "Sleep tight."

"If I can sleep at all," she said.

He grinned, because he knew it was going to be a problem for him, too. "'Night." He dropped a kiss on her lips, then turned to leave.

"'Night," she echoed, watching him go.

And then the door closed.

Sighing, she fell on the bed. She was in love with Rafe. It was all over but the screaming. Softly, she laughed at herself, at him, at the world. Oh, what was she going to do?

Chapter Nine

It was nail-biting time, but Rafe wasn't thinking about that. He'd really wanted to win the competition, but recently he'd discovered he wanted something more. He wanted Shelley.

The feeling was growing inside of him and he couldn't stop thinking about it. He liked women. He liked dating. He liked flirting and having other intimacies. But he'd never wanted a woman for his own, to be with him for the rest of his life—never, that is, until now.

Actually, she'd been around most of his life. She'd been a part of his life almost from the beginning. And now he wanted to make sure she stayed there, permanently and firmly. He wanted guarantees, because for some reason, he suddenly couldn't imagine life without her.

This morning he found himself walking in the gentle radiance of that new realization, smiling at everyone he met. He was feeling good. *Like I'm drunk on love,* he thought to himself. It sounded stupid—but it sounded right.

At breakfast, Shelley sat across the table from him and he couldn't concentrate on anything but her. The sunlight streaming in from the tall windows behind them turned her hair to gold. Her slow smile and almond-shaped eyes made his blood dance in his veins. She was so familiar, and yet, so new. And he wanted her more than he'd ever wanted anything else in his life.

It looked to be a long morning. After breakfast the team congregated in the conference room—going over last minute details, running through the items again and again and trying not to get too nervous. They were scheduled to be one of the last teams to perform. In the meantime, they had to sit and wonder how the others were doing. They were allowed to go and watch some of the other teams put on their submissions if they wanted to.

"I can't even imagine doing that," Candy said dramatically. "I'm sure everything I saw would make me feel like we were doing it all wrong, and then by the time our turn came I'd be a wreck."

Rafe had to agree with that to some extent, but he was feeling so restless, he had to get out and move.

"I'm going to take a walk," he said to the group, though everyone immediately understood whom he was talking to. "Anyone want to come?"

Shelley looked up and he caught the warmth in her eyes as they met his. He knew she felt the same way about him that he felt about her. Unless he was crazy. Unless he was misreading everything. If he could work up the courage to follow through—if he could work up the nerve—this was going to be a good thing.

"I can't go right now," she said regretfully. "I promised Dorie I would go over her lines with her one more time. You go ahead. Maybe I can meet you later."

He strolled out into the main hall, luxuriating in the glow of this new feeling. It was so new he still marveled at it. He'd never thought he would have anything like this. He'd never understood how men he knew suddenly felt they wanted to have one woman only for the rest of their lives. But now he knew. He had that feeling, too. And he knew that was what had been missing from his life.

He passed near one of the halls where the competition was going on and he paused, looking in. There was Jason McLaughlin on the stage. This had to be the McLaughlin Management entry. He shook his head. This ought to be good. Silently he slipped into the hall and took a seat near the back.

It only took a few moments for him to realize they were doing his idea. There it was, right on the stage. Jason was playing the part he should have been playing, directing the others in preparing to lobby hard for circumstances conducive for a winning bid on the Quarter Season Ranch.

At first, he couldn't believe it. His mind kept trying

to find reasons this couldn't be true. But he finally had to admit it to himself. They had stolen his idea. How could that be? Turned to stone, Rafe sat perfectly still, staring at the stage and unable to look away.

Shelley took a short turn out into the lobby, hoping she would catch a glimpse of Rafe somewhere, but he was nowhere to be seen. Instead she found Quinn coming her way. His hair was combed off his face and his clothes looked clean and pressed. Funny how little things like that could make such a difference in a man. Today, he looked like someone worth knowing.

"Quinn!" she said. "Good to see you again. How are you?"

"I'm okay, I guess." He stopped to grin at her, his hands shoved down into the pockets of his jeans.

"Did you come to watch the competition?"

"Yeah. Matt told me to come and right now, I'm doing whatever Matt tells me to."

"Good thinking." She smiled at him. "Listen, weren't you in a band in the old days? How's the band going?"

He gave her a quizzical look. "The band broke up over a year ago. I've been getting a few gigs on my own. Now and then." He shrugged, looking away. "Things are a bit tight in the music world right now."

"Oh. Well. Have you thought about trying something else?"

"No." He frowned at her as if she just didn't get it. "How can I do something else? Music is my life."

She offered him a smile. "If your life keeps trying to starve you to death, it might be time to start thinking about dumping it for a new life."

She could tell by the look on his face that he didn't much care for her advice.

"Well, right now my life is going to change anyway." He grimaced. "I'm going to get stuck in that little po-dunk town, Chivaree."

"Hey, I'll have you know Chivaree isn't so bad." She almost laughed aloud to think that she was the one saying such a thing. Defending Chivaree, imagine that. "It's grown a lot lately. We've even got a new TidyMart."

"Hey, that's exciting."

"And some big box stores, and the latest in fast food cuisine drive-thrus."

"I can tell I'm going to feel right at home."

She made a face at him. "Your sarcasm is uncalled for, Quinn. I think you're really going to be surprised at how much you like it in Chivaree."

"Yeah, maybe." His eyes brightened. "Hey, Shelley. Sorry about ditching you the other day." He grinned at her suddenly. "That was some driving you did. I thought you were going to catch me for a moment, there."

"I still don't get why you were avoiding me that way."

"Listen, you never know. Those gangsters I was run-ning from are smart. They could send you or someone like you in to trap me. I couldn't take the chance. I've been ditching everyone for weeks."

"Well, they haven't caught you yet. You've still got your legs."

"Yup, still got 'em. With Matt helping me, I might be able to keep 'em."

She laughed and let him go on in to look for Matt. Surveying the room, and then the hallway, she still didn't see Rafe. Frowning, she went back to join the others.

The McLaughlin presentation was over. People were leaving, and Rafe still sat where he was, thunderstruck. He could hardly believe what he had just witnessed. How could this have happened?

The ranch sale prospect had been leaked to him in confidence by a very close friend who was involved in the proceedings and had authorized him to use it if he wanted to. Therefore he knew no one else knew about it except those on the Allman A team. And now, it seemed, someone on the McLaughlin team.

Jason had spotted him and was coming his way. Then he was standing in front of him, smirking with obnoxious triumph.

"How did you like it?" he asked, looking malicious. "Did you think I did your idea justice?"

Rafe just stared up at him and didn't answer for a long moment. "Who told you?" he asked at last, his voice hoarse. "Who gave you that plan?"

Jason's grin got wider. "I can't really tell you that. I wouldn't want to get her into trouble. But I think you know who I'm talking about, don't you?" He shook his head. "I've always had a special bond with this woman. There's just something between the two of us that won't be denied. She tries, of course. But when I ask her for something I need, she gives. She's all about giving, isn't she?" His eyes gleamed maliciously.

Rafe still couldn't believe it. It couldn't be true. And whether it was true or not, he wanted to kill Jason anyway. So he started up, ready to go after him, but someone grabbed his arms from behind.

"Hey," Matt said, appearing just in time to stop him from doing something very stupid. "I don't think that would be a good way to earn any points for the team, do you?"

Rafe turned on him. For once in his life he was furious with his brother.

"Leave me alone," he ordered, shaking off Matt's restraining hands.

When he turned back, Jason was gone. Glaring at Matt, he left the room as well, heading out into the street. He had to get some fresh air and get this dead feeling out of his system.

It was time to go on stage. Shelley's knees were knocking but she forced herself to ignore that. She was going to do a good job of this if it killed her.

"Where's Rafe?" she said urgently. He hadn't come back from his walk and that had been over an hour ago.

Candy shrugged.

Shelley went to the door and looked out into the

larger hall, only to find Rafe's sister Jodie and her fiancé, Kurt McLaughlin, coming toward the conference room.

"Jodie!" she cried, glad to see the woman who had been her best friend since early childhood.

Laughing, they hugged and looked at each other as though they hadn't seen each other in ages instead of just a few days.

"I can't believe you came for this!"

"Well, Kurt and I were sitting there at your mom's café having breakfast and wondering how things were going here and, all of a sudden, Kurt said, 'Why don't we just go and see for ourselves?' So we took the kid over to stay with Rita and here we are."

"I'm so glad you came. I just hope we don't make you sorry."

"Don't even think that way. You guys are going to do great."

That was the hope, but things were so nerve-racking now that Shelley couldn't really think straight. All she knew was, it was time to present. Looking around she saw with relief that Rafe had finally showed up. Then, moments later, they were marching into the hall, ready to take the stage.

All in all, the team was pretty happy with the way things went. The skit went off great. Candy didn't fall down and nobody knocked over any scenery. The VCR worked fine and the piece of videotape went over well.

As the moderator, Shelley started the presentation off. She stood to the side as the invisible narrator, explaining what was going on, interspersing a few jokes, which actually elicited a few laughs. Candy was great as the program coordinator and Rafe was convincing as the traditional skeptic who was won over in the end.

They wrapped it up and the judges left. And they hugged each other in relief and happiness that the ordeal was mostly over. Shelley looked around for Rafe and, when she found him, she threw her arms around his neck and gave him a hug as well. Even with all the talk and laughter around them, she noticed that his reaction wasn't all she could have hoped for.

But there was no time to ask him about it. They were due in the auditorium for the awards ceremony and they had to hurry over. The teams had been assigned to seating areas and they were all given pompoms with their team's colors on the way in. As leader of her team, Shelley had to direct the cheers. Even those were a part of the competition, and she did her part with suitable enthusiasm. When she returned to her seat, she found herself sitting between Jaye and Candy. Rafe was sitting two rows back with his brother and sister, and when she looked back, he didn't seem to notice her.

She was getting a bad feeling and it was growing. Something was wrong and there was no way to get him alone to find out what. The first speaker was funny and the second told a touching story of faith and hope, but Shelley didn't hear much of either. All she could think about was Rafe and his sudden coolness. Was it just because the weekend was ending and he wanted to get back to normal? She couldn't believe that. Not after the way they had connected last night.

Finally it was time for the awards. They sat on tenterhooks as the moderators started with tenth place and slowly worked their way toward the top. Jason's company won fifth place. But when second was called and it still wasn't Allman Industries, the tension was so taut it almost killed them all. They held their breath.

"And first place, for the best exploration of the theme of trading places with the boss, goes to…Allman Industries!"

They went crazy then, jumping up and down, whooping and hollering. They were actually going to take that huge trophy back to Chivaree with them. It was a wonderful moment. Shelley and Rafe went up together to accept the top prize, and they each made a short statement. And for those few moments, they were both grinning from ear to ear.

They had already reserved a banquet room in the hotel dining room for their end-of-competition party and all started heading that way, pushing their way through the crowd to get there. Shelley took a detour to her room to freshen up a bit, then took the elevator back down and started for the dining area. And there, standing at the checkout desk with his bags in tow, was Rafe.

She headed right toward him.

"Where are you going?" she asked him in amazement. "We won! Don't you want to celebrate?"

He turned to look at her, his dark eyes remote. "I've got some thinking to do," he told her.

She went very cold inside. "What do you mean?"

He shook his head. "Don't worry, Shelley. It's just me. I've got to think some things over. Get my head straight. It's a long drive back to Chivaree. I'll have a lot of time to do it." He gave her a fleeting smile, picking up his bags and turning toward the entry. "Talk to you tomorrow," he said.

And he was gone.

Shelley stood staring after him. Something had happened. But what?

Hurrying to the dining room, she sought out Matt, who was talking to Jodie.

"Rafe has gone home," she told them. "What's wrong?"

Matt looked surprised, then swore softly. "Oh, that idiot. He shouldn't let it get to him like that."

Shelley shook her head, still puzzled. "Let what get to him?"

"You haven't heard? Jason McLaughlin's team did what I guess was the idea Rafe wanted to do with your team. He sat there in the audience and watched them do it. He seemed pretty upset."

She frowned, shaking her head. "I still don't get it."

"The plan about preparing a frontal assault on getting hold of Quarter Season Ranch?" Jodie explained. "It seems Jason's people put it on pretty much the way Rafe had meant to do it. It was obvious to him that someone gave them the plan."

"Oh, no!" Shelley gasped, knowing that would infuriate Rafe. She wished she could go to him. Why hadn't he told her? "Oh, my gosh. No wonder he's upset."

"If it had been anyone but Jason McLaughlin…" Matt said, shaking his head.

"But they didn't win," Shelley pointed out. "They didn't come anywhere near winning. We won." She thought for a moment, frowning worriedly. "Well, I can understand why Rafe was angry. But why do I get the impression that he's blaming me?"

Matt shrugged, hesitated, then told her point blank. "From what I gathered of the conversation I heard, Jason implied he'd obtained the whole plan for the presentation…from you."

She froze. "From me?"

"He didn't?" Jodie said quickly.

"No." She shook her head, frowning with bewilderment. "I never breathed a word of it to anyone."

Jodie shrugged, though she looked relieved. "Well, let him go stew for a while. He'll come back to his senses soon enough."

Shelley was torn. Part of her wanted to go after him—but that was pretty silly. She wouldn't find him until she got back to Chivaree. Besides, she couldn't leave. She was still the boss until the end of the conference and she had the other teammates to think about. So she joined the others in celebrating and tried not to think about Rafe.

Of course, that was impossible. But the more she thought about him, the more she got a little angry herself. He didn't really think she would betray him that way, did he? If he did, he had no faith in her at all. That didn't sit well. In fact, she was getting downright furious about it.

Still, she was determined not to let Rafe's actions dull the pleasure she took in the win. After all, this was a credit to her to some extent. And she was proud of it. She'd proved that she could do things that she hadn't thought she could do. She was sure that her life was going to take a turn for the better after this. Unless…

Unless Rafe decided he couldn't stand her after all and never wanted to speak to her again. A queasy feeling swept through her at the thought, but she pushed it away. She just couldn't believe that could happen. They'd been so good together!

She wasn't going to let anything destroy this day. Pasting a smile on her face, she joined in the general hilarity and tried to have a good time. She would think about Rafe later. She wasn't going to be a victim of circumstances this time. She would think of something.

Chapter Ten

Rafe had a sick feeling in the pit of his stomach as he turned his car onto the highway. He hated that horrible empty feeling. It reminded him of something but he didn't know what. He frowned, trying to place it. Whatever it was, he didn't want to go there.

Suddenly he had a flashback to the way the house felt, the way his stomach felt, the day of his mother's funeral. That was it. A swell of nausea hit him and he cursed, fighting it back. He wasn't going to let himself feel this way. There was no reason for it. This was nothing like losing his mother. Nothing else had ever hurt so much and nothing ever would.

Still, he knew now what it came from: trusting, caring, believing and having all those things thrown back

in your face. In other words, betrayal. Loving and losing. Or something like that. Where was little Miss An-
alyze Everything to dig the truth of this out of him?

Maybe he'd been right to hold off the way he always
had, to protect himself. If this was what you got when
you opened yourself up, he wasn't sure it was worth it.
Suddenly the words of wisdom he'd heard years before
from a friend echoed in his ears.

"If you don't want your heart broken, don't fall in love."

Words to live by.

Good thing that hadn't happened yet. Good thing
he'd been forced to come face-to-face with the reality
that Shelley might not ever be able to love him the way
he would need her to—if he did fall for her.

He didn't want to think about Shelley. And yet, he
knew she was all he was going to think about all the way
back into town. Pressing down on the accelerator, he
headed for home.

"Ah, forget him," Candy advised with a wave of her
hand as they stood in line at the hotel checkout, ready
to pack up their cars and turn toward Chivaree. "Men
are all the same. Don't take any one of them seriously.
Two-timing louses."

Shelley stopped. Something inside her was rebelling.
Candy sounded very much like the things she used to say
herself. But this wasn't like that. Rafe wasn't like that.

*Oh, stop it! You've been wrong before, haven't you?
What makes you think you could be right this time?*

Yes, she had been wrong before. But she'd learned something here this weekend. She'd been put in the position where she had to try to do something she didn't think she could do. And she'd done a pretty darn good job of it. If she hadn't tried it, she wouldn't know it was possible. She wouldn't know how far she could go.

She'd chickened out before. She'd turned and walked away when things got tough. How would she ever face herself again if she did that now? No. She had to reach out. She wasn't going to give up on him, not this easily. If she truly loved Rafe, she had to go after him. Even if she was risking everything to do it.

She said goodbye to Matt before departing. "I hope this works out, you bringing Quinn to Chivaree," she said. "I hope he doesn't disappoint you."

Matt shrugged. "That's really not the point," he said. "I just want to do what I can to help him. And in the meantime, he might be able to help me more than he knows in finding my baby."

"So you're seriously looking?"

Matt nodded. "I've got to. That baby is out there somewhere and I have to make sure it's being cared for."

She understood that and thought all the better of Matt for it. But she was afraid his search was going to be long and lonely.

"And Shelley," he said, turning back and smiling at her warmly, then giving her another bear hug. "I don't think I've thanked you for finding Quinn and doing all you could to help me. I want you to know how much I appreciate it."

"No problem," she said, her eyes misting. "I wish you all the luck in the world."

She drove back to Chivaree with Jaye Martinez riding along. The B team hadn't placed, but they'd had a lot of fun and Jaye gave her all the details all the way home. She was talking so much she didn't seem to notice that Shelley barely said a word.

Her mind was racing, thinking over all the angles. It was all very well to make plans to go after Rafe—but if he hated her now for something she hadn't done, maybe he wasn't worth pursuing. But she refused to believe that.

When you got right down to it, there might be more than met the eye. There was her past, after all. Maybe he'd finally digested what she'd done, how she'd been with Jason when it was so wrong. Maybe he'd come face-to-face with the whole picture and he just couldn't accept it. Maybe he'd decided she wasn't worth the effort or the emotional currency.

Maybe—if she didn't want to risk being cut to the quick by finding out what he really thought of her—maybe she ought to leave well enough alone and just accept things as they were.

But she couldn't.

She ached to see the light of pure affection in his gaze again. She loved the man. And she wanted him to love her.

But she wasn't desperate. No, sir. She'd learned a lot this weekend. She'd done a good job and she was darn proud of it. She'd proven her worth to herself. Never again would she feel the need to find some man to hang her life on, the way she'd tried to with Jason.

She certainly wasn't looking for another Jason to undermine her self-confidence.

Oh, yeah? a little voice in her head said mockingly. *Then why'd you go ahead and fall in love with Rafe Allman?*

"Because he's different," she muttered aloud. "He's worth fighting for." Then her mouth tilted in a tiny smile, because she knew she was right.

Monday morning in Chivaree usually meant a cup of steaming coffee at Millie's Café, and that was where Rafe ended up.

Millie greeted him with her usual friendly smile as he took a stool at the long counter. Most seats were filled and the place buzzed with casual conversation. The smell of coffee and bacon filled the warm air. Millie took his order from the other side of the counter and he leaned close as she wrote down his request for a bagel and a cup of black coffee.

"Hey, Millie," he said as she started to move away. "Did you know I spent the weekend with your daughter?"

"You did *what?*" she demanded, swinging back to face him, her still-pretty face registering astonishment.

He gave her his slow grin. "We were both at the conference in San Antonio," he said.

"Ah." She relaxed. "I didn't think it could have been

anything more romantic," she admitted. "You two have been at each other's throats all your lives. I can't count the number of times she came home when she was a kid, yelling about 'that darn Rafe Allman' and whatever you'd done now."

"'That darn Rafe Allman.'" He nodded, smiling ruefully. "Yup, that's me."

Millie obviously needed to get to other customers, but she lingered, looking at Rafe as though she could read the edginess in him. "What's the matter, honey?" she said. "Somethin' got you spooked?"

He smiled at her, but instead of answering, he asked, "You knew my mother pretty well, didn't you?"

She reached out and touched his arm with a soft hand that managed to convey understanding along with sympathy. "The two of us didn't see much of each other in those last few years, but there was a time when we were real good friends."

Rafe stared at her. Why had he brought this up? He wasn't sure. But she seemed to find it a natural enough question.

"I always thought her going so soon affected you the most," she said musingly. "You were her special one, you know. And when we lost her, you seemed to pull back into a shell for the longest time." She shrugged and smiled at him. "I'm so glad you finally found your way. From what I hear, you're doing real well at that business of your father's."

She ruffled his hair as though he were still that little boy.

"I know your mother is looking down right now and she's real proud of you," she said, a slight catch in her voice. With a quick smile, she turned to get him his coffee.

He watched as she drifted on to serve coffee to someone else. She moved with sure and steady charm, topping off one customer's cup, stopping to say a word to another. What exactly had he wanted from her? Sympathy? She'd given that. She always had. Despite the animosity that sometimes simmered between him and Shelley, he'd often looked to Millie for a little mothering in the old days. Funny how easily you forgot those things as you grew up and left childhood behind. He hadn't thought about that for years.

He shook his head ruefully. Millie was a nice lady but her daughter was messing with his mind right now. He should find a means of forgetting about her. There had to be a way.

"You look like a man who could use a piece of pie."

He looked up, startled, and found a new young waitress with the name "Annie" on her label pin standing over him, waving the aforementioned pie. It was cherry and she'd added a little mound of vanilla ice cream for good measure.

"Uh, no, thanks," he said, shaking his head. "I didn't order pie."

"I know that, but honestly, this one's left over," she said, plopping it down in front of him. "It won't fit in the display case. I thought you might like it."

He gazed at her quizzically. Her dark hair curled out about her pretty, friendly face and her protruding stomach showed that she was about six months pregnant. "I can afford to buy my own pie, you know. If I should want some."

She made a face. "Boy, talk about looking a gift horse in the mouth. You're not very good at accepting favors, are you?"

Her smile was infectious, but he was resisting. He was, after all, in the middle of his great dilemma. Was he or was he not going to try to have a relationship with Shelley? "I've got thinking to do here."

"Thinking goes better with a piece of pie." She pushed the plate more solidly in front of him. "What I know from experience is this—a man who looks so sad while he's thinking could use a piece of pie." She nodded knowingly. "And I also know that he's probably thinking about things he said to his woman, and how to get back into her good graces without losing too much of his dignity." She shrugged and leaned toward him over the counter. "I've got one word for you, mister," she said confidentially. "Red roses."

She was persistent. He had to give her that. He wasn't sure if it was an endearing quality—or just plain annoying.

"That's two words."

"But one concept."

"True." He gave her a twisted grin. "How do you know I was the one in the wrong?"

"Are you kidding?" She turned to go. "Does it matter?"

"What do you mean? Of course it matters."

She looked back at him, hesitated, then gave him one more piece of advice. "This isn't likely to be a situation where logic and justice apply. The only thing you need to think about is—how are you gonna make her smile?" She shrugged. "Red roses."

With one last arch look, she was gone. But Rafe hardly noticed. He was having an epiphany.

He was an idiot.

Of course, that wasn't news, but in the current situation he hadn't realized just how stupid he was. Here he'd been angry because Jason stole his idea and put it on at the conference, and he'd been resentful of old ties Shelley had with Jason. All that had him all tied up in jealous knots. And he thought that was his problem.

But that wasn't it at all. He knew damn well that Shelley hadn't given his idea to Jason. And she'd proved to him again and again that she didn't want anything to do with the man. So what was his problem now? He was just acting like a big baby, wanting the whole world to shower him with some sort of sympathy. Wasn't he?

And why was he letting himself devolve into this infantile state? Fear. Pure fear. And an excuse to set himself up to be left behind again. He glanced up toward the heavens. Millie was sure his mother was up there, looking down. What the hell—maybe she was. Just to be safe, he smiled for a second. And felt a flood of warmth and well-being.

"Hi, Mom," he mouthed. Then he picked up a fork and started in on the cherry pie.

It was almost an hour later when Rafe strode confidently into the lobby of Allman Industries and met his sister Jodie coming out of the personnel office.

"Hey, where've you been?" she said. "Pop's here and he's been holding court up in the boardroom, congratulating the team and gloating over the trophy. He's happy as a pig in a new load of Galveston mud. You ought to go on up there and join in on the general festivities."

He grimaced. "If I must," he told her.

But he did want to. He took the ancient elevator up and got off at the top floor, then met most of the team going the other way.

"Hey. Is it all over?"

"Pretty much," Candy said, grinning at him. "But Shelley's still in there with your old man. Where were you?"

"I got delayed."

"You gotta get in there and see how good that trophy looks in the middle of that table. *Hoo-eee!*"

"It's going to look even better in the trophy case," he told her.

She frowned. "What trophy case?"

"The one we're going to build."

Her face cleared. "Oh. Right." She grinned as he went on toward the boardroom.

He pushed open the door. His father was sitting at the

head of the table. Gaunt and gray-haired, Jesse Allman still had the look of a force to be reckoned with.

"Hey, Pop," Rafe said, sliding into a chair to his right. "I hear you're pretty partial to this old tin can we brought back for you."

He glanced at Shelley, hoping to read in her eyes what she was thinking, surprised at the way his heart was thumping at the sight of her. She was standing, holding a stack of folders to her chest, as though she was about to go. But her eyes were shaded and he couldn't see a thing there. He looked away, heart sinking, and hardly heard his father at first.

"Yeah, that's one beautiful trophy y'all won," Jesse Allman was saying, nodding at Shelley approvingly. "I'm a happy man today, I can tell you." He grinned, his gold tooth flashing. "Good thing I got Matt to go down and help y'all out. That was the smartest thing I ever did. You can always count on Matt to come through."

Shelley stiffened, glancing quickly at Rafe, then away again. Should she say something? No, it really wasn't her place. But if Rafe was just going to let this go…

"Hold on just a darn minute, Pop," Rafe said to her surprise. His expression was casual, benevolent, but she had a feeling there was something less benign going on under the radar. "Where'd you get the idea that Matt had anything to do with this?"

"I sent him down there, didn't I?"

"Sure," Rafe said slowly, his gaze meeting hers for only a second, then moving on. "And having him show up was a morale boost, no doubt about it." He hesitated, then charged on. "But he was taking care of some private business and he wasn't even there until he came at the end to watch us put on the performance. The rest was all up to one person." Rafe turned and looked at Shelley. "And you're lookin' at her right now."

Jesse looked annoyed. "Well, I know she did a real good job. I thanked her plenty and I told her she's gettin' a bonus, just like all a' them."

Rafe shook his head, his jaw set, his gaze holding hers. "Not good enough."

Jesse frowned at his son. He wasn't used to being contradicted by anyone, much less one of his children. "What the hell you talkin' about, boy?"

Rafe wasn't going to be intimidated by his father's usual temper. "I'm talking about the fact that Shelley Sinclair took charge, fought me off, brought in a killer idea and pulled off a show-stopper of a submission to the competition. She showed every characteristic of a damn good manager."

He was still holding her gaze and she was breathless.

"She's getting more than a bonus," he went on confidently, "she's getting a promotion. And we're darn lucky to have her working for us."

Shelley was tingling with the praise. Having her hard work recognized would be wonderful. But somehow bittersweet. And suddenly she realized that she would rather have one warm and loving smile from Rafe than all the bonuses and promotions in the world.

"Well, okay," Jesse was saying reluctantly, his brows knit. "That's good. I'll talk to Matt and see if he knows somewhere we can use her."

"No," Rafe said, his voice low but strong. "I'll take care of it."

Jesse reared back. "Now you just hold on. I'm the president of this company…"

"And I'm basically the CEO." He finally tore his gaze from hers and looked at his father. "And I'm making a command decision. I want Shelley in charge of research and development planning."

"What? She's not qualified for that!"

"Pop, it's my decision." He rose and stood beside Shelley. "We're going to go now and talk it over. I'll present our offer to her and see if she accepts it." He put a hand on the small of her back and began to escort her out of the boardroom. "I'll let you know if she takes the position. See you, Pop."

Jesse was muttering something malevolent but they didn't stop to hear what it was. Shelley's head was spinning. She was glad Rafe had finally let his father know he wasn't going to take his browbeating with a shrug and a smile any longer. That was a very good thing. And she was gratified that he was thinking of new positions for her. She'd been working toward that for a long time. But that still didn't resolve things between the two of them, and when she looked at his face, she couldn't see anything there that reassured her. She knew now that he wanted her promoted, but did he still want her in his arms?

They took the elevator down to the floor where her desk was, along with five other women in the section. Rafe talked quickly, outlining what her new position would require and sketching in the duties and new pay schedule. Shelley nodded but she only half heard what he was saying. It was a fabulous offer, of course. Better than she'd ever dreamed of. Better than her ambitions had allowed her to think of. And she was going to turn it all down.

The elevator came to her floor and they stepped out, pausing in the empty lobby.

"Well?" he was saying. "What do you think? Does it sound like something you would be interested in?"

She looked up and searched his face. He really did think this was going to make up for everything, didn't he? He would hold out this reward, this wonderful chance, and she would take it. They would be even. He wouldn't have to worry about her anymore. He could go on as though nothing had happened between them this weekend. He wouldn't have to open up his heart and commit to anything. No risks.

She knew about that. She'd lived a lot of her own life the same way. But it was no good.

"It's a fantastic opportunity," she told him. "But I can't take it."

"What are you talking about?"

"I can't work here with you."

He frowned, running a hand through his dark hair. "Shelley, I thought we'd worked through all that old garbage…"

"We did. This is new garbage."

She tried to smile but it was a weak effort. Here it was. Did she have the courage to do this? Was she going to reach out and take her chance, or let it slip away?

Taking a very deep breath, she squared her shoulders and held her chin high, meeting his dark gaze with her own clear eyes and praying that her voice wouldn't break.

"You see, Rafe, I'm...I'm in love with you."

His handsome face registered shock, crushing her. He hadn't expected this, had he? And if he loved her, even a little bit, would it have been such a surprise?

"I think you can understand that it would be impossible to work here with you under the circumstances. I mean, since you don't love me."

He took her by the shoulders, staring down into her face. "Who says I don't love you?" he demanded, his voice strangely hoarse.

"Well, I thought..."

"You've got to cut me some slack, Shelley," he said. "I've never been in love before. I'm just feeling my way here."

A delicious sense of hope shivered through her, but she held it back, still too wary to let herself believe in it. He'd only said he wasn't sure—hadn't he?

"So, you're thinking that maybe...?"

He frowned down at her, troubled but strangely elated at the same time. There was no getting around it. He could try as hard as he might, but he couldn't stop himself from loving her. He knew it had to be love because it felt so ridiculous—and there didn't seem to be anything he could do to stop it.

"No, I'm not saying 'maybe.' Shelley, I can't think about anything but you. I dream about you at night. You fill my head and my heart like no woman ever has before. All I want is to be near you. All I think about is how to make you happy. I've got to think that it's love."

She was laughing softly, shaking her head. "Either that or a bad case of the flu," she said lovingly. Her heart was singing. "But I'm ready to risk calling it love if you are."

His large hands cupped her face. "I don't have any choice," he admitted, feeling helpless, looking helpless. "Shelley, I love you."

With a cry of joy, she threw her arms around his neck and he held her tightly, raining soft kisses on her pretty face. Then his mouth found hers and their kiss deepened, growing as their love ignited the passion that was lurking between them.

The elevator doors opened and suddenly Jesse Allman was there, glaring at them as he began to make his way into the lobby, his cane tapping.

"I said it was okay to promote her," he grumbled. "You're taking this a little far, aren't you?"

They pulled apart and Rafe grinned at his father. "I'm taking it all the way, Pop. I'm going to marry her, or die trying."

Jesse harrumphed and went on his way. "Better check with Matt before you get yourself into anything you can't get out of," he said back over his shoulder.

Shelley gasped and looked at Rafe, but he was laughing, so she joined him. She was just too happy to let anything mar the feeling right now.

"Come on," he said, pulling her back into his arms. "Let's go someplace where we can explore this new love thing and all its ramifications without being interrupted."

"Okay, boss," she said, touching his face with her fingertips. "You lead the way."

"Oh, wait," he said, reaching into the pocket of his suit coat. "I forgot to give you this." He pulled out a bedraggled red rosebud with a rather crushed and broken stem and handed it to her. "It was the only one I could find in this whole darn town."

She took it gingerly. "Where did you get it?" she asked.

He looked a bit embarrassed. "Remember Mrs. Curt, the fifth-grade teacher? Her yard. And I had to fight her aged bloodhound to get back out of that place alive."

Shelley laughed. It looked a bit the worse for having been banged around in his pocket, but it was still a beautiful shade of red.

"Why?" she asked him, shaking her head.

"I was told it was required," he said innocently. "Don't you like it?"

She looked down, biting her lip. "I love it," she said, her voice breaking. She knew she would preserve it forever as a token of this wonderful day. Looking up, she gave him a radiant smile, her eyes misting with unshed tears.

He nodded, satisfied. "I guess it works after all," he said. "It's supposed to symbolize something." He realized exactly what as he was talking. "My heart," he said as the thought occurred to him. "It's yours."

She held it close, smiling lovingly at him. "Thanks," she said. "Now that's an offer I really can't refuse."

* * * * *

In May 2005, from Silhouette Romance, watch for Raye Morgan's delightful conclusion to
BOARDROOM BRIDES.
In this third installment, a mesmerizing M.D. gives his very pregnant secretary a hefty dose of TLC!
Will **THE BOSS'S SPECIAL DELIVERY** *bring wedding bells to Chivaree?*

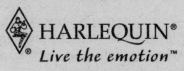